Wildwoods and Wishes

Wildwoods and Wishes

SUSAN BERENCSI

DOUBLEDAY & COMPANY, INC.

GARDEN CITY, NEW YORK

1981

All of the characters in this book
are fictitious, and any resemblance
to actual persons, living or dead,
is purely coincidental.

Library of Congress Cataloging in Publication Data

Berencsi, Susan.
Wildwoods and wishes.

I. Title.
PS3552.E696W5   813'.54
ISBN: 0-385-17317-2   AACR2
Library of Congress Catalog Card Number 80–3007

First Edition

*If ever there's a time
to express love,
and gratitude . . .*

*for Zoltan,
my loving husband*

*for John and Bette Shullick,
my wise and wonderful parents*

*for Cora Henriksen,
the dearest of friends*

Wildwoods and Wishes

CHAPTER 1

Eve of Spring, 1799

"Git a move on or I'll blast ye's ta hell," bellowed the coachman. With a deft flick of his wrist he uncoiled the leather whip with the speed of a striking serpent. The earsplitting retort intermingled with heavy plodding hoofs and echoed ahead of the coach, slamming against stalwart tree trunks before reverberating farther down the muddied lane.

The travelers crossed a narrow gully lined with clumps of beech trees and staghorn thickets. An arboring tangle of branches muffled the noise from the wheels churning the thick liquid underfoot.

It was difficult for the horses to hold their footing. The mares were drenched with spattered mud and nasty enough in temperament to equal the lackey's rankled disposition. They were on the verge of bucking free of the rigging in order to sidestep the quagmire sucking in their hoofs.

Irritated by the slow progress and at his difficulty in handling the skittish nags, old man Decker cursed himself for not asking a higher fee for his services. He was barely thankful for the shillings jingling inside his moth-eaten pocket.

Decker called himself a fool for carrying the gentry to and fro on such a miserable day. Indeed, the girl passenger inside was not his idea of a blue-blood! His own bugger eyes be damned if he didn't see her clutching those wet-nosed urchins at the minister's house; acting like a common nursemaid. What was worse, the other passenger was a fat ol' wench, whose tongue had lashed at him like a fishmonger's wife. Decker vowed not to waste his time to play the footman for these two!

"T'was bad enough ta'kin tha ol' stuffed sausage to tha vic'rage to fetch 'er ladyship," he muttered to himself, "but to be put to work in this slop when oiee kin be sippin' ale at Mother Ziggy's Tavern is askin' too much!"

He spat on the sodden wood brake handle when he thought about his lack in comforts. Frustrated and spiteful, he slapped the reins of wet leather against the horses' rumps and caused them to lunge ahead, jerking the coach and weary occupants before they went waddling onward.

Thin waves of blowing drizzle moistened Sundra Bradford's face when she dared to peek from the shelter of the window shade. Sundra was curious and wondered how long she would be jostled before they reached the landmarks leading to Bradtree Manor. She'd been sent away from home to reside with the Reverend and Mrs. Wells for three months past, and her family never once thought about her until now. She was perplexed by the sudden posthaste in her return and could not imagine why her father had hired this coach instead of sending one of his own. And why was her father's message written by her stepmother?

A charge of lightning made Sundra back away from the window. The storm was making her nervous. She snuggled against the hard leather seat, her lithe body making a shallow dent in the cushions, slender arms holding the flaxen tassel for support.

"Come now, Miss Sunny. I've been awatchin' you fret and fidget and it won't do you any good! Try to rest yourself a bit. Listen to your old nanny, child. Haven't I always known what's best for you?"

With a bobbing motion, Addie tucked the lap rug securely around her mistress. She awkwardly returned to the opposite corner and dropped her ample figure on the seat, deliberately causing the coach to lurch in her direction. Overhead, Decker stomped his boot on the boxed boards, his gutter language overpowering the distant rumble of thunder.

With her eyes tightly shut, Sundra sadly remembered departing the home of Reverend William Wells and his wife Grace, who had guided and tutored her periodically from toddler to grown woman of ten and seven as more than just a favor to her widower father.

Other than her most recent visit, Sundra had not stayed with the childless couple for nearly a year, during which time they had used funds secured from an endowment and had expanded the clergy house into a foundling home. The Wells's eagerly gave their love and care to the multitude of bastard babes and deserted youths cast aside because of family shame or poverty. Sundra sympathized with the little ones and openly gave her heart to them, feeling their loss of parental love through her own recent sufferance of rejection.

Sundra took a deep breath and sighed as she recalled the only serious argument she ever had with her father. She had taken an immediate stand against his intentions to wed Lady Miriam Mace. Sundra was somewhat covetous of her father's love, having lost her mother at birth, but would have relaxed her feelings had he chosen someone other than her dreadful third cousin.

Deep inside her heart Sundra knew her father would not have the serene home life he should be enjoying during his elderly years if he were to wed such a persnickety firebrand.

"I don't think Miriam is the woman who could make you happy," Sundra stated innocently.

"Such silly prattle!" Lord Giles said reproachfully. "Why can't you be as conscientious about Miriam's welfare as you are for the servants, hmmm?"

"But . . . she tyrannized the staff behind your back!"

"Pah! Servants need a firm hand now and again. Besides, I'm beginning to think you're jealous," retorted Lord Giles, contemptuously.

The words slapped Sundra in the face. It wasn't true! She tried at all cost to make her cousin feel welcomed at Bradtree, but the results were always the same—fruitless. Miriam's demure facade would soon disappear unless everyone gave her their undivided attention. It was Sundra who always wound up forgotten in the background, but never once did she ever complain or begrudge the fact.

"But, Father," she pleaded as a last resort, "we're close

enough in age to be sisters. Why surely you can't . . ." Sundra
was startled into silence when her father's hand slammed down
hard upon his desk. A pink blush spread over her diminutive
face, feeling ashamed for wanting to discredit Miriam, who was
not present to defend herself.

"I may or may not be an old fool, Sundra. Do not push me
into thinking that my only child would dare to question my actions. 'Tis not of your nature to act this way. So until you come
to your senses, young lady, I forbid you to speak about this
subject any further," ordered Lord Giles, pouring a liberal
amount of brandy into his glass. He could not make his daughter understand the reason why a man his age strove to marry a
much younger woman.

Lady Miriam Mace soon became the second Baroness of
Bradtree, and did not waste time in packing Sundra off to the
country vicarage to tactfully ensure a fruitful adjustment pe-
riod for everyone.

"Miss Sunny, please wake up. We're almost home!"

Slowly Sundra became aware of traveling on the rickety
planked bridge crossing over to the estate. The subsiding storm
had left a heavy dampness clinging to the gray surroundings,
creating a spiritlike mist to blanket the limp strands of unshorn
grass with tiny crystal beads. The odor of decayed wood seeped
in through the windows as they passed under a tall arbor of
walnut trees shielding a vacant groundskeeper's cottage. The
grounds had been neglected during Sundra's absence and, as the
horses kicked up fragments of crushed cinders along the last
winding curve of their journey, the untended appearance
caught her attention.

Sundra reluctantly left Addie to gather her personal baggage,
which had been carelessly thrown down from the rack. She entered the hall and was disappointed no one awaited to greet her.
"Father, I'm home," she called out. "Miriam? . . . Is anyone
here?" She felt as though she had entered a closet filled with
stone-cold silence and stagnant air. Depressed, she walked alone
to her room, half expecting to find cobwebs lacing her doorway.

Sundra barely had time to wash her face when a forceful knock resounded on her door. The thin servant, dressed in a dark brown sacque and stiff white apron, entered without permission and fixed her impenitent eyes on Sundra.

"I'm Mrs. Iris Reed," she said crisply, "the new housekeeper. My lady wishes to see you in her sitting room."

"Yes, of course I'll see Miriam right away. But I've traveled all day in this dress and I must hurry to change it. Would you please help me get it off?"

Sundra wearily turned around and lifted aside her cascading curls, an unusual shade of chestnut veined with sparkling gold strands, so the woman could unfasten the tiny loops on her dove-gray frock. The kersey wool material was damp and had sorely chafed her delicate skin.

Mrs. Reed cocked her head and raised a bushy eyebrow, her face remaining the color of tallow melted with frown lines. "Your own maid can assist you later on, missy. 'Er ladyship wishes to see you now!" hawked Mrs. Reed, marching away.

Sundra entered the sanctum of Miriam's boudoir. The interior was illuminated by the fire, flaming shadows dancing on the flocked wallpaper which still smelled of flour paste.

She hesitated in greeting her cousin. As always Miriam looked stunning, and even more so wearing a new cremosin dress trimmed with costly bone lace.

Sundra brushed a speck of mud off her sleeve, painfully aware of the contrast her soiled traveling outfit made against the grand decor. Would Miriam once again titter at her modest attire or begin to downgrade her for excelling in her studies as she so often had in the past?

"You're a dowdy little mouse and always shall be!" Miriam had often heckled her when they were blossoming into womanhood.

Sundra mustered her courage to confront the self-proclaimed paragon poised across the room, wishing all the while she had gone straightaway to speak with her father instead.

Miriam broke the tension in the air by quickly moving with graceful strides toward Sundra. She breathed a sigh of relief as she gingerly embraced the girl. A welcoming hug was the last gesture Sundra expected.

"Thank goodness you're home safe and sound! Oh, Sundra, it was a terrible mistake for me to have sent you off to the Wellses' in the first place. If you only knew what I've been through . . ."

Miriam captured Sundra's arm with a cold grip and fainted backward onto the love seat, pulling the girl down with her.

"Miriam," gasped Sundra, alarmed to see her suddenly looking so pale. "Let me help you. Here, breathe deeply," she ordered gently as she revived Miriam with her vinaigrette.

"Thank you," Miriam replied feebly. "Oh, what must you think of me! It may please some people to know that I am being punished for all of my misdeeds right here and now."

Miriam paused to wipe her tears and blow her nose, allowing Sundra to unconsciously place a comforting hand across her own.

"Why now of all times," she cried, shaking her head. "My marriage to Giles has made me a better person. I've even prayed for another chance to earn your kind friendship, although I wouldn't blame you for shunning me, now that my world is collapsing . . . We're poor, Sundra, and your father is very ill because of it."

Before Sundra could utter her disbelief, Miriam launched into a detailed account of their problems and household changes. Lord Giles had made a succession of heavy investments which failed, causing his funds to diminish at an alarming pace. The family was financially ruined and the baron sank steadily deeper in debt trying to recoup his loss. Giles was losing his health as fast as he had lost his sizable fortune.

"Even if Giles were to sell this estate and all of his possessions, we would remain in debt," whimpered Miriam.

"How can this be?" questioned Sundra. "Oh, my poor father! Miriam, how did you manage all this time when Father was laid up in a sickbed?"

"I'm sorry to say that his prized horses had to be sold at the local market. We couldn't afford to send a groom to hawk them at Tattersall's."

Most of the staff had been dismissed, explained Miriam. Addie had been loaned to a neighboring estate rather than retire her without compensation.

"I parted with my double carcanet of pearls to buy back Addie's services from the Wilkes family," sobbed Miriam. "I wanted her to be with you again."

Sundra's brow wrinkled in consternation, feeling guilty to have held a childhood grudge against Miriam for causing havoc in their earlier years. Now was not the time to harbor resentments toward anyone, including Miriam. Sundra had never seen her cousin looking so devastated or brokenhearted.

"Miriam, let's forget about the past," pleaded Sundra. "If you could forgive me for objecting to your marriage, I too, would be most grateful to give our friendship a second chance. But first, I'm overly anxious to hear about my father. Is there anything I can do to help?"

"Giles is worried that he'll soon be taken to debtors prison, regardless of his weak heart or title. I insisted on seeing you first, my dear, because you are the only person who's in a position to help him. Think about Grandfather St. Ives's legacy to you and what it could mean."

An extravagant dowry awaited Sundra as bequested in the unusual will written by her maternal grandfather. The only stipulation was purely sentimental. Sundra would inherit, provided she would repeat her marriage vows on the traditional St. Ives wedding date. What year she would choose did not matter —until now.

"Since you've refused gentlemen callers in the past, your father had no choice but to arrange a marriage contract for you," Miriam said quickly. As though to make up for her bluntness, she gave Sundra another awkward hug. "Don't look so startled, dear heart," cooed Miriam. When she did not receive a response, she added subtly: "A sweet, innocent girl like you would never forgo her family obligations, would you?"

A marriage of convenience was the last thing Sundra wanted, but if Giles Bradford's life and well being depended on her actions—"I promise to do whatever my father sees fit in order to unite our family during troubled times," vowed Sundra. "Whom did he choose for me?"

"'Tis Sir Elliot Spencer!" chortled Miriam. "You met the baronet at my wedding reception, remember?" She assured Sundra that Elliot was much in favor of giving financial support to Lord Giles in return for his daughter's hand.

How could I forget, thought Sundra in dismay. Elliot had dressed like a peacock, ogled the women when his mother wasn't watching, and had guzzled as much rum punch as his rotund belly could hold. But he was polite, and she supposed the choice could have been worse—but not by very much.

"I am honored and must thank him for his generosity," stammered Sundra, her romantic heart quailing with reluctance. She looked forlornly at her cousin for reassurance.

Miriam smiled with tears in her eyes. "Go assure Giles with a brief visit, my dear, but don't be shocked by his faulty speech or useless limbs. Smitty will tell you when to leave."

Miriam shut the door and listened to Sundra's footsteps fading down the corridor. She picked up her skirt and skipped across to her dressing table where she quickly dabbed her pale cheeks with Spanish papers until they blushed seductively red. Before sneaking away from her room, she stepped with a vengeance on top of a snuff box decorated with a miniature of Lord Giles, crushing the delicate fragments into the parquetry.

As the next morning's sun nudged through the mist, Sundra was huddled on a marble bench in the private garden watching filtered beams lighten the rolling terrain behind the gray-stone manor.

She hadn't been allowed to visit her father for more than three minutes, or question him about his matchmaking decision. Lord Giles, on the other hand, had looked relieved and satisfied to hear about her forthcoming marriage.

All the years of daydreaming about a love match had been in vain, she thought. It was the dowry necessary to save her family which must take precedence over all else—including her futile wishes for love in her future.

CHAPTER 2

The days passed swiftly, leaving the Bradtree household in a disarray of harmony and a mixture of emotions. Lord Giles remained a withered and tormented man confined to his feather-bed. He constantly cursed his legs for not being able to move him away from the foul sickroom sprinkled with powders and littered with pomanders to purify the air.

Whenever the baron became excited, his breath would wheeze and fall in short gasps. Occasionally, he was rational in thought, but his messages would always come out garbled and shock the ears of his few listeners. What words he could expound were left choking in his throat. His mind remained in control until the physician's elixir took effect and befuddled his brain.

"Ah yes, Dr. Mortley," he mused with detached interest. "Why that pompous bag o' sawbones! No better than all the rest of those jackanapes waiting to line their pockets with gold!"

It no longer mattered to Lord Giles that his good reputation was scoffed at by the beau monde. He hated to think about the small fortune he had spent on lavish banquets and fancy routs just to induct Miriam into London's society; fanciful whims he had never bestowed on his genteel daughter.

Matriarchs vied with each other to be seen in the company of the wealthy new baroness. But after the news of his financial downfall spread like wildfire, the Bradfords were immediately ostracized from their circle.

Lord Giles's precious letter of introduction to Almack's was literally torn up in front of his face. Remembering this brought back all the insults and indignities he'd had to contend with ever since.

The clink of glassware interrupted Lord Giles's thoughts. Smitty was dexterously measuring the liquid potion into a beaker without spilling a drop.

"Good day, m'lord," he chirped. " 'Tis of the hour for your medication."

The valet tried to sound cheerful, knowing his master did not take kindly to having the brew forced upon him.

"Bahh!"

Lord Giles heaved from the thin and gritty syrup sticking in his craw. He turned away in disgust. Smitty leaned over to perform the never-ending chore of wiping sputtered drops from his master's chin and prepared to take his leave. The baron tossed his weakened arms as a sign for the servant to stay. Smitty longed to remain and help relieve Lord Giles's ennui, but he risked losing his employment if he ever went against Lady Miriam's strict instructions—no visitations! He left the room in sadness to resume his watchful post outside the door.

Lord Giles's chest grew taut from his piqued condition. He started to perspire. He became lightheaded and knew the bitter concoction was bringing about another stupor. He curled his lip to think some good had come from his heart's malady; it kept his wife away from his bedside! Miriam was indifferent to another's suffering and cared only for herself. The vixen turned out to be wicked and far craftier than he would have believed possible.

He might be bedridden and useless, but he needn't worry about not being able to protect his daughter from Miriam. Just when he feared for Sundra's well-being, she had confided to him about consenting to a marriage with Sir Elliot Spencer.

Lord Giles knew very little about the baronet, but, knowing his daughter's dream for a love match, trusted her judgment in choosing a husband. He couldn't understand what she saw in such a dandy, but still, he breathed a sigh of relief to know she would have a man to protect her.

Addie maintained a reserved attitude toward Miriam even though Sundra had thrown all caution to the wind by placing her faith in her cousin.

A flux of newfound duties imposed by the baroness kept Addie's hands tied. Her tasks of drudgery kept her from aiding Sundra, who felt obligated to follow Miriam's erratic schedules day and night.

The maid was irked to find Sundra bending over backward to please the baroness when the girl should be playing fancy free like the other young maidens.

Miriam was always popping up out of nowhere to catch Sundra unawares. She would then shilly-shally, taking Sundra with her to make linen inspections because she did not trust the depleted staff. The poor girl frittered away many afternoons just to help the baroness choose an outfit to wear. Because Miriam professed a dire need for Sundra's companionship, the girl set aside her precious textbooks in order to be at Miriam's beck and call.

Sundra would search for Addie whenever the tensions of the day proved too difficult to cope with. Granted, she was displeased with her maid for voicing objections against her marriage commitment, but she couldn't stand by to watch Addie brood for days and suffer because of her promise. Sundra loved her nanny dearly and could never stay at odds with her for very long.

Addie was more than willing to boost Sundra's morale, restoring her famous sunny disposition with her glib tale about the first time Sir Elliot paid court. His appearance alone was worth a hidden look of doubt and a restrained smile from Sundra, who knew enough about fashion to know it had changed.

Sir Elliot apparently preferred the old styles because his hair was powdered white, no matter the occasion, and his silk breeches were flowered with gold.

The coup de grâce came during his elegant bow, bidding farewell to the ladies. He tripped head over heels from the heavy leather overshoes he was wearing and landed on top of the fern baskets, smashing them into smithereens.

"Oiee! Now that, was a sight to see," guffawed Addie. "I had it in me head to tell him it was a wee bit too early in the day to be in his cups!"

"Elliot was nervous, Addie," explained Sundra. "He's been trying very hard to win my affections. Why, Miriam told me he asked Father's permission to bring over his horses, knowing my passion to ride through the woods and clover fields."

The baronet faithfully traveled the fine highways of London to the rutted dirt paths of the valley at least twice a day to call on his intended, making good use of the short time they had to become better acquainted before their wedding. They took prancing rides in the morning, with Miriam acting as chaperone, and afterward parted company to attend to their private affairs before the occasion of afternoon tea brought them together again.

Eventually Sir Elliot was invited to stay for all evening meals at Bradtree. His abundant thirst for port wine made up for his lack of appetite during mealtime, when he merely pushed tiny portions of food against the back of the fork tines, being rather fussy as to what filled his stomach.

After dinner the trio would settle in the front parlor. The simple, elegant interior had been changed recently to suit Miriam's taste in decor. Sundra felt ill at ease with the bold red flocking and outlandish brocades but never mentioned the fact to her cousin. She knew Miriam was trying her best to replace the worn furnishings using a limited purse.

"I want to please Giles," Miriam would often whisper to Sundra, "because I love him so."

Sundra would lower her eyes, thankful her father had a wife who was totally devoted to him. She would play Elliot's favorite ditties on the harpsichord. If he ran out of wine he would station himself close beside her while waiting for another bottle to be brought in. Sundra never faltered from the heavy aroma of spirits on his breath, valiantly trying to adjust to the idea of a close contact with him; a familiarity which would lead to more intimate terms. Miriam always sat nearby. Watchful. Sundra couldn't have asked for a better chaperone.

On several occasions, when Sundra couldn't fall asleep, she had gone to Miriam's room to talk or to bring her a cup of hot chocolate as a friendly gesture. Miriam's chambers had always been deserted.

The third time Sundra couldn't locate her, she was going to alert the staff when she caught Miriam sneaking back to her room.

"I'm afraid you've caught me, Sundra!" Miriam had whispered in a high pitch, her fingers toying with a vial of laudanum hidden inside her pocket. "You see, my dear, even though I have restricted visits to your father, I am guilty of violating my own rule. I need to kiss him good night, whether he's asleep or not. You'll understand what I mean once you become a married woman and know the joys of true love."

After that night, Sundra never left her room. She was afraid she might infringe on the privacy Miriam and her father shared late at night. Any further explanations on Miriam's part would only cause embarrassment.

Sundra grew bored with the monotony of daily routines. She wished to spend her precious moments with her ailing father, whom she was still restricted from seeing.

Lord Giles might fare better if she could share her sentiments about obeying her wedding vows. The splendor of her daydream wedding had been cast aside. She accepted the reality of an impending marriage brought about by necessity and contracts instead of love.

Eight days remained before the nuptials were to take place. Miriam took complete charge by attending to the details of the informal service in all phases. She hired a postchaise to take Sundra and her maid into London to shop for a wedding dress, a last-minute surprise gift from her to the bride-to-be.

"Good-bye, Sundra! Remember, something new and something blue, and I'll have a sixpence for your shoe." Miriam sang the words off key. What better way was there to involve Sundra more deeply in her trumped-up friendship than with a debt of gratitude for a new dress!

Miriam turned her back and snickered. It was like giving sweetmeats to a babe! She had limited the gold coins on purpose, making sure Sundra could not afford to purchase one stitch of clothing that would threaten to outshine any of her own.

Sundra's meager wardrobe was dainty and tasteful but rather plain. Miriam did not want to take the chance of the girl splurging on herself. Lord knows how miffed she'd been because Sundra, even though she possessed limited gifts, had the ability despite herself to make a gunnysack look absolutely fetching.

Sundra patronized Madame Rene's shop all morning with fittings and careful selections of trimmings for her limited trousseau. The seamstress was most cordial. She was elated her budgeted handiwork could heighten the appeal of the petite one, who not only possessed sea-green eyes and hair of rich luster, but an inner beauty of the soul as well.

The woman took the soft satin slippers, petticoats and chemises of gossamer, ribbons and hairpins and set them in boxes. The pelisse of sage-green silk and the high-waisted white muslin dress trimmed with tambour embroidery was placed into containers lined with lavender-scented packets.

Sundra was very pleased with her purchases, neatly stacked in a high pile and held firmly by Addie. They went in search of the carriage, rounding the busy street corner in anticipation of returning home to admire the new clothes.

A woman screamed to no avail as Addie collided with the lady's tall gentleman companion who was equally burdened with boxes, sending the parcels flying in all directions.

"Of all the nerve! How dare you bump into us like that! Just look what you've done," lashed the woman, who bore a striking resemblance to Miriam. She pointed her long fingernail at the delicate nightgown strewn over the grimy cobblestones.

"See!" she hissed, tossing her head in a way that made her black ringlets look like bouncing snakes. She snatched the transparent blue gown from the gutter and shook it in front of Addie's nose. Angrily, she tore off the bow, flinging the dirtied piece at the maid's face.

Sundra and Addie were embarrassed and shocked at the sight of a personal garment being waved about in public, and at the woman's venomous attack.

"Now, Alice," calmed the man, whose chin was set and eyes were cast with warning flashes between amused glances. "Your gown is not ruined. Why, it barely had time to touch the ground before you snatched it up."

"But the ribbon! I wasted a great deal of my time, and patience, to make sure Marie altered the gown to my taste. What good is it to me now?"

"It will look best without it. Let us not waste our time, or delay these ladies," he growled impatiently, tipping his tall hat in Sundra and Addie's direction as though he had just noticed them for the first time.

"Piffle!" shrilled Alice. "The bow of lace is ruined and I certainly wouldn't want to be humiliated wearing the gown without it! Here," she raved as she tossed the delicate garment at Addie, who humbled herself for the sake of her young mistress and voiced her apologies. Addie's reward was a pooh-poohing from Alice, who saucily walked away.

"You can squeeze into it and pop the stitches for all I care. Keep it with my best wishes, you troublesome baggage."

Alice spit out the words loud enough for the passersby to overhear. A few eyebrows were raised; their noses turned upward as they skirted past Addie. "You deserve what you get," was written across their smug faces.

Addie controlled her temper. She had never cared for the likes of the highty-tighty social flits in the past and she wasn't about to waste her time on them now. No one could get the best of Addie Quiggs unless she let them.

Sundra was shaking and nearly in tears as a result of Alice's cruel tantrum; a perfect example of why she didn't want to be part of the pampered society she was being forced into by marrying a wealthy baronet.

Sundra looked up, startled to see Alice glowering at her. Their eyes locked. She felt the stab of green-eyed jealousy. Alice was livid with rage as she stood defensively beside her carriage, mindful that her companion's attention was focused elsewhere.

"Don't contaminate yourself with these country milkmaids,

m'lord. 'Tis enough I'll have to air out these pretty things you bought for me, on account of them! Now, take me home!"

There was no response from her gentleman. He silently cursed at the boxes he was gathering while his eyes leisurely feasted upon Sundra's comely figure.

Alice cooled her voice into a taunting murmur to distract him from his preoccupation. "You have a delightful way of making me forget my anger, eh, m'lord?" she dared to purr, leaning back against the carriage door, knowing full well her suggestive pose would embarrass the innocent-looking young girl.

Sundra held her chin high and walked over to face Alice, determined at the same time not to make a spectacle of herself which might cause shame to her family or Elliot.

"Yes, madam, my maid and I are from the country," spoke Sundra, very calmly, "but we are not milkmaids. Nor do we have to be in order to recognize a bovine when we see one staring us in the face."

Without waiting to see Alice's reaction, Sundra blindly rushed back to the corner and made a wild grab for one of her parcels. She bumped into the handsome gentleman with such an impact that he was forced to drop his packages in order to save her from falling.

Once Sundra regained her balance she tried to back away from the stranger. He didn't let go of her arm. Instead, he teasingly pulled her closer against him, amused to see the rosy blush on her cheeks darken into crimson patches.

Sundra's eyes flashed green fire in response to his wide grin, which only prompted him to tease her all the more.

"I'd wager my matched bays that you would look far lovelier in the negligee than Alice Rose," he baited her with an intimate whisper. "Had I the time . . ."

"You, sir, can take your horses and go straight to the devil himself!"

Sundra whirled away from him. She darted back to Addie's side. While hurrying toward their coach, she glanced over her shoulder and threw a dagger look at Alice's gentleman.

He smiled and winked at Sundra. His eyes remained

transfixed on her body, lingering his gaze on her engaging backside.

Sundra was infuriated by his bold stare. To show her disgust, she contorted her face and grimaced at him. Untypical of her character, she practically shoved Addie into the coach. Sundra's petticoat snagged on the steps, adding to her humiliation during her hasty retreat. "Oh dear," she thought aloud. "What's come over me!"

Once settled, she dared to peek out of the window. The man was still smiling in her direction. He was unable to hold his composure at her antics and threw back his head, laughing heartily. As the coach pulled away, Sundra could see Alice pummeling his chest in a fit of jealousy.

"Keep away from that window," warned Addie, "or else he'll know you've been staring too! A flagrant man if I e'er saw one! Imagine, him flirting with such an innocent girl like you, and his trollop standing within earshot to boot!"

Sundra was too bewildered to have noticed Addie tucking the expensive nightgown into her carpet satchel. Try as she might, she could not forget the piercing cobalt blue eyes of the stranger looking at her from head to toe, shamelessly lingering his gaze upon her lips, her neck and the blossoming shape of her body! No man ever dared to scrutinize her with such a beguiling but brazen manner.

"I'm glad to leave this city, Addie, and I hope never to lay my eyes on him again!" Sundra claimed rather curtly.

"Now mind you, Miss Sunny. I still don't approve of you marrying Sir Elliot, but, 'tisn't proper for a girl who's about to be wed to let another gentleman affect her thoughts or her heart!" Addie admonished her.

Sundra shivered with goosebumps. All the way home to Bradtree she chided herself for thinking about the nameless stranger, his handsome face and virile manners, who should mean nothing at all to her.

Sunday morning was a time of bustling activity as the aged staff retreated to the village for a day of rest. They weren't eager to begin cleaning twenty-five rooms, polish the splintered parquet floors, and wax the huge cherrywood panels, or decorate the manor with ivy for a marriage ceremony which no guests had been invited to attend. Smitty and Addie, alone in the world, remained behind in their humble quarters.

Sundra was happy to be living at home again, being near her father even though he remained in seclusion, and enjoying Miriam's hospitality. Slowly, she was feeling confident about her future. Besides, it was too nice today to brood about the inevitable anyway.

She watched Sir Elliot's carriage pull up to the front entrance. His lackeys were bedecked in uniforms of chartreuse silk with frilals and gold buttons. They were always fidgeting, which made the large plumes on their tricorns bob up and down. Sundra wondered why they were constantly ill at ease in the company of their employer.

Elliot came to deliver a large bouquet of glasshouse lilacs for Sundra. Since Miriam was not available to act as chaperone, his visit was brief. Before departing he ventured a bold kiss upon Sundra's hand. His tongue flicked across her reluctant wrist to sample her sweetness. She couldn't bear to look into Elliot's puffy little eyes.

Sundra was left standing alone in the portico, wiping off with revulsion the traces of Elliot's slobbery kiss. She was shaking because he had relished seeing the shocked look on her face when he had touched her.

But she knew it was unfair to hold Elliot's eagerness against him. She too had felt the excitement from stolen affections from the stranger in her dreams. With a dreadful feeling, she knew she could never love Elliot under any circumstances and be satisfied and fulfilled at the same time.

Sundra shuddered to think about her obligations when Elliot would claim her on their wedding night. She could imagine what Addie would say to her right now: "See what good your silly wishes for a love match got you?"

The handsome face of the arrogant stranger from London flashed in her mind. The memory of his searing eyes, the sensations she felt when he held her close against his body, would forever haunt her conscience. Drat him! Sundra grew angry and confused. Heaven help her, she was frightened by her innermost thoughts.

CHAPTER 3

Sundra focused her attention on the bouquet of flowers as she inhaled the assuaging fragrance from the tiny purple buds.

After searching the dusty storage rooms she found a porcelain vase and wiped it clean for her arrangement. She rushed toward the back staircase built with heavy planks and plain hewn boards of honey-colored oak.

Sundra skidded to a halt when she came face to face with her father's valet. "These are for Father," she told him gravely. Smitty blocked her path and frowned at her for trying to use the servant's passageway. He stifled the lecture he was about to reprimand her with, knowing she was desperate to see Lord Giles. But should he allow it?

"Good day, Miss Sundra. Do let me assist you, please."

"Thank you, but no. I, uh, I would like to take this up to Father myself. Oh please? I won't stay but a minute." Sundra pleaded with her eyes. "I miss him, Smitty. It's hard for me to stay away. Why, I don't even know how he's feeling."

Smitty rolled his eyes and hesitated a second before choosing a reply. "M'lord has been very restless and perturbed, even a trifle insistent, if I may be permitted to say so. The window, of all things, was bothering him. He ordered me to leave his chambers. 'Tisn't like him at all! So, I'm going to fetch a spot of hot basswood tea to refresh his spirit."

Smitty saw the look of concern in Sundra's eyes. No harm done in an unscheduled visit with her father, if he were to look the other way. "I'm not certain Lady Miriam will understand why I let you, but . . ." He gave Sundra a nod of approval and tactfully excused himself.

Sundra mounted the squeaking staircase two steps at a time.

The vase was poised so the water couldn't spill out as she hurried down the corridor to her father's room. She slowly opened the door, determined to avoid the noise of a creaking hinge which might disturb him. She tiptoed past the rosewood entryway and stopped dead in her tracks!

She was spellbound at the sight of her father being out of bed. He was balanced between a chair and the oriel. She was further silenced by his sudden movement, watching his elbows bend and strain as he positioned his wrinkled and feeble body aside the window mullion.

Sundra gasped. Her father's legs looked twisted from pain. He was crying! Within seconds the gentle shaking of his shoulders turned into spasms of violent tremors which sent him sprawling to the hardwood floor.

The vase shattered on the planked boards as Sundra screamed. She crushed the delicate flowers underfoot as she rushed to her father's side. His face was ashen. His lips were turning blue as he fought for breath. Sundra was attempting to raise his head when Smitty came rushing into the room with Addie close on his heels. The maid took one look at Lord Giles and firmly pulled the girl away to allow Smitty to get near his master.

"We'll see to his lordship, Miss Sunny. Ye best be sending for the doctor to come at once." Addie scanned the opened window and upturned furniture. She fingered the hem of her apron as she nudged Sundra toward the door. "Ye better fetch Lady Miriam too, but I don't want to see the two of you going into hysterics! Now calm down and get going."

Sundra ran from the room on shaking legs. Her search to find Miriam in the house was to no avail. She bolted out of the manor and worked her way throughout the front grounds. She spied a draft horse and bumpkin rider trodding into view. Through weeds and nettles she kicked up the long folds of her skirt as she quickened her pace to reach the road before they passed by.

"Louie! Louie, over here! Hurry!" she called, waving her arms high in the air. The stablehand from the neighboring estate trotted over to her. She gave him the urgent message to find Dr. Mortley, which sent the lad off at full gallop.

Sundra did not stop to clear her thoughts, hysterically darting back to the gardens to continue her search for Miriam. Thinking that her father would need his devoted wife by his side more than ever, she vowed never to forgive herself if she failed to bring him the one comfort he should have during his time of need—a wife's loving care. She commanded her legs to run faster.

Sundra instinctively chose a short cut and went racing down an old footpath leading to the back veranda where Miriam could often be found having midmorning tea. Intent on throwing back a low-lying branch blocking her way, she misjudged her footing and went tumbling down alongside the lichen-covered stairs of pitted limestone. Sundra made a desperate attempt to try and stop her fall by grabbing the dark green myrtle edgings. She uprooted the plants instead, hanging onto the fistfuls of black humus and gnarled roots as she rolled roundabout toward the bordering hedges. She came to an abrupt halt when her head slammed into an iron post rail.

She lay breathless and stunned on a mossy patch of damp earth. She was dizzy. Exhausted. Her heart was thumping heavily inside her chest. When she tried to raise her head, the surroundings appeared dark and hazy. As soon as her sight returned to normal, the blurriness would come back to torment her. She curled up on her side. Sundra was about to give way to tears but stopped when Miriam's tinkle of laughter pricked her ears. The ground space between the yews revealed a sight which made her doubt her own convictions.

Miriam and Elliot were clinging together in a flushed appearance of obvious delight. She tilted back her head to expose a long, slender neck for Elliot's parade of kisses. When his wandering hand started taking liberties with Miriam's protruding breasts, exciting him to press closer against her body, Sundra lowered her eyes. She knew what was taking place and was revolted by the sight.

Miriam slipped away from him and swayed her hips in a

seductive manner. The baronet was agog for Miriam's delights
and awkwardly reached out to recapture her in his arms.

"So! You think to torture me, eh?" purred Elliot. "Come
near me, my lovely minx! I must hold you, touch you, for I can
never have my fill of you. Miriam!" he pleaded. "The memories
of having you grace my bed these past months are not enough!"

Miriam took Elliot's pudgy hand and pressed her lips against
his bejeweled fingers, satisfied that her captivating maneuvers
had enslaved his body and soul. She coaxed him over to the secluded area of thick yews where Sundra lay hidden from their
view.

Sundra held back her labored breathing. She had a growing
desire to flee and risk discovery rather than remain a witness to
their lovers' tryst of betrayal. She tried to block out their words
as they came nearer. Suddenly, Sundra heard a slap and a loud
grunting moan. Gripped by fear, she remained paralyzed on the
cold, musty ground.

"Come now, Elliot! We must be careful," hissed Miriam,
silently damning the shrewd tone of her warning. The amorous
spell had been broken.

"Oh, come now yourself!" puffed Elliot. He wiped the thin
rivulets of sweat from his brow, allowing his lustful fire to cool.
His mouth trembled. He swallowed the lump of barbed jibes,
knowing if he didn't quell his temper, he'd live to regret it.

"It's my nerves," Miriam reasoned quickly. "We've come too
far with my plan to risk discovery this late in the game. If
Sundra ever got wind that it was I, and not her father, who had
arranged her marriage . . . or why Giles is penniless . . ."

"Don't go off on a tangent," interrupted Elliot. "You've seen
how complacent Sundra's become with her lot. Do you think
she'd act that way, knowing you had tricked her? Or, that you
gambled away Giles's fortune? There's no cause for alarm, my
dearest," he encouraged her. "I congratulate you for concocting
such a fabulous tale about the baron's bad business ventures.
Heh heh! You've a fine nose for sniffing out money. I wonder
what poor Sundra would have done if she had seen you in ac-

tion at Bootles after the ol' chap closed the establishment for the
night? Shaking your derrière under the gaming tables when you
scrambled to search for lost coins that some drunken lout had
the misfortune to lose. Why, hee hee . . ."

"Oh, for heaven's sake! Stop reminding me!"

Elliot cautioned her against losing her sense of adventure.
"Giles will never receive a pence from his daughter's coffers, I'll
grant you that!" he declared smugly. "Once I have my way
with the chit, she'll do all of my bidding very nicely."

"Don't forget who put you in that position, Elliot! By rights
that dowry should have come to me first, regardless of what the
courts ruled," remarked Miriam, seething because Grandfather
St. Ives had excluded her from his will—and she an orphan too!
She swore she'd have her cake and eat it, and had married Lord
Giles as the first step in her quest for money and revenge. "We
can thank our lucky stars that Giles's heart is weak. The opium
you gave me makes it easier to keep him sedated, but we're not
out of the woods yet. Just keep doing as you're told and you'll
get your share of the dowry."

Miriam was winded. She wasn't pleased to be hashing over
her plans when it brought to light another problem to contend
with. Sundra had declined the Wellses' invitation to visit with
them after the wedding. This meant the lovers couldn't have a
free hand to dally, with Sundra underfoot.

Elliot pursed his lips. A sinister chuckle arose from the depths
of his throat. "I have my ways to keep the servants from gossiping," he simpered. "Who's left to tell her about us?"

"Sundra has eyes and ears of her own! So don't let her helpless angelic character fool you. She'll suspect something is
wrong the very moment we even think of throwing Giles in the
poorhouse."

Elliot didn't want to waste these precious minutes with
Miriam on problems. He was hungry for more kisses. "We'll
force the little dove to flee our love nest somehow or else we'll
have to do away with her permanently," he said abruptly. Already the embers were starting to rekindle his flame for pleas

ure. He so urgently wanted the chance to nuzzle the swells of her flesh that he could almost taste it. Hand in hand, they sauntered toward the shadows of privacy in the dilapidated gazebo.

Sir Edmund Dillingham obligingly fetched the lard from the pantry and walked thief-in-the-night fashion down the corridor until he was safely inside Sundra's room. He gave the small wooden firkin to Addie.

Working on the commode, Addie mixed oils of juniper and amber and poured it into the fat. She added a few drops of seneca oil. The last of Barbados tar was spooned into the concoction which would ease the swollen bruise on her mistress' head.

For the first time in his life the barrister was at a loss for words. He never expected his dear friend to die so suddenly. Not Giles, he moaned. To heap misery atop woe, Edmund blamed himself for adding the crushing blow upon this sweet girl whose life deserved better.

Sir Edmund was nervous. His throat was parched. Ugly red blotches were covering his face this very instant as he tried to confront the maid. "How is the poor girl!" he croaked.

Addie did not take the time to answer him.

"Dear me! When I accompanied Dr. Mortley over here, I had no idea whatsoever to expect. Well, after I had finished talking with him, I came downstairs. Lo and behold! I saw Sundra crying alone in the foyer. Naturally I presumed that she already knew about her father's death. Curse me! I should have waited before I blurted out my condolences. She collapsed at my very feet before I could say another word to her."

Sir Edmund started to pace back and forth. He needed a drink. If the maid didn't start talking to him soon, he would run out of the room to find one. "I'm to blame, you know. I caused her to fall and receive that nasty wound on her head. Perhaps I'd better fetch Mortley in here before he takes his leave."

"Please, Sir Edmund!" Addie replied hastily. "'Twill be all right." She secretly worried about what took place to make Sundra disheveled and battered long before Sir Edmund ever laid eyes on her. She had been on her way to meet Sundra, watching her stumble up the front stairs, when the barrister appeared on sight. "Dr. Mortley is a very busy man. We should not infringe upon his time when there's nothing left for him to do."

Addie did not want the ferret-faced doctor to come near the girl if she could help it! She knew enough about healing to doubt his methods, also disliking him because he paid more attention to Lady Miriam on his visits than he did to helping Lord Giles.

"You're not to blame yourself for Miss Sunny's accident. I'm grateful that you were on hand to assist me in helping her, and I will tell her of your kindness when she awakens. But, not a word about this to anyone, eh? There's no need to have folks upset at a time like this," suggested Addie. "Come along, sir."

Addie wiped her hands on her apron. Quietly, she gathered the jars into the basket and left the room with Sir Edmund. She settled the lawyer in the study and made certain he had a full decanter of port to keep him company.

She then found Lady Miriam in her sitting room, performing the duty of condolences to the widow who openly mourned for her departed husband. Assured that her services were not needed at the moment, the maid hastened from the room with renewed determination. Addie puffed as she worked her way back toward Sundra's secluded chambers.

Sundra remembered very little about how she had returned to her room. She rubbed her hands and arms in the darkness, feeling as though she was coming out of a drugged sleep.

The tapers were not burning and she felt too exhausted to get up and light them. She was surprised to have slept into the night, especially since she did not have the peace of mind to aid her slumber; grieving for her father in her nightmare of reality. She knew he had suffered the Grim Reaper's fatal blow because he had witnessed the garden tryst from his window that she too had stumbled upon minutes later. Her agony over a fool's errand and subsequent sorrow left her drained of all tears and energy.

Sundra touched the sticky lump on her throbbing temple and winced in pain. While shaking her head in self-pity she tried to sit up to arrange the feather pillows which lay crushed beneath her body. She reached behind her back and raised her legs as she swung aside the pillow. The quilt pulled loose from her straining legs, throwing her off balance. Her shoulder came down against the edge of the mattress at an awkward angle which caused her to flip over backward onto the floor.

The girl crawled forward in the surrounding darkness to pull her body free from the tangled bedding. Velvet folds of drapery brushed against her tousled hair as she positioned herself against the wall. Sundra felt miserable and confused, her green eyes were red from spent tears. She reached for the drapes and drew them side to allow the cool evening breezes and shafts of moonlight into her stuffy room. Her limp curls were suddenly lifted away from her face by an updraft of tepid air. She also heard the chirpings from active birds!

Sundra froze and held her breath until her heart started pounding its way to her throat. Wildly, she made a grab for the curtain lining and ran her fingers across the fabric, feeling the warmth of the midday sun upon it. Sundra let the material slide away from her hand as she realized she was not dreaming. She was blind! The revelation overcame her senses and she began to scream.

Addie found Sundra floundering in the middle of the room with a wild stormy-sea look within her eyes. The maid used all of her strength to subdue the mere slip of a girl and settled her down upon the nearest chair. Kneeling beside her, Addie comforted Sundra within her plump, motherly arms.

Wisps of angel-hair clouds webbed the sky by the time Sundra regained control of her emotions. Slowly she told Addie the details of what had happened to her from the time she had left her father's room until the moment she discovered her blindness.

When Addie was informed Sir Elliot was a pawn, a willing participant, in Miriam's quest for Sundra's dowry, she held back the I-told-you-so lecture. Knowing she had been right all along did not give her as much satisfaction as she first thought it would.

"How cleverly cruel of Miriam to use Father's mute state to aid her scheme," whispered Sundra. "Who knows what she was doing on those nights I couldn't find her."

"Probably feedin' his lordship with a spoonful o' lies and bad medicine, rest his soul. But what about the baroness' gambling? Even if she had lied about the debts, m'lord was too smart of a man not to have known about it. Why didn't he try to warn you about her!"

"Oh, Addie," cried Sundra. "I can't bear thinking that maybe he did want to warn me, only we never had the chance to communicate. Miriam and Elliot's liaison surely must have dashed his last wish to see me safely wed."

"Er, now, Miss Sunny, we've talked enough. I shouldn't have let you go on about this until I had a chance to look at your eyes. I'm going to fetch some herbs and soothing patches right now. I'll put the light back in your eyes, just you wait!"

"Please hurry," begged Sundra. "If Miriam or Elliot were to find out I'm blind, there's no telling what they'd force me to do next. I don't have to marry Elliot, but if I don't escape from here soon, I'll be at their mercy!"

"Raise that proud chin, Sundra Bradford. You'll not be a prisoner to those wicked dregs if I can help it," pledged Addie, pushing up her buxom chest so her large frame stood straight and imposing. She handed a hairbrush to Sundra and told her to put it to good use. "Stay put until I return," she added, "and don't let anyone come in here."

Miriam came caterwauling into the room before Addie could leave Sundra's side. The baroness held a pure white handkerchief next to her powdered face, dramatizing the effect of the puffy redness around her soggy eyes. The maid shot her a sarcastic glance when she wasn't looking. Addie thought that Miriam must have peeled some bloody onions to have achieved the huge teardrops.

"He's gone," wailed Miriam with a snort. "We share a great sorrow to have lost . . ." she stopped short, nearly choking on the words as she gawked at Sundra's profile. "What's happened to your head?"

Addie felt Sundra stiffen with fear. She gave her a quick pinch, cluing her to remain tight-lipped in Miriam's presence.

Sundra spoke the truth by saying she had collapsed after she heard about her father's death, omitting the fact of having the whopping lump on her head well beforehand. She sensed Miriam was scrutinizing her appearance. She made a half turn in her seat so her cousin couldn't see her blank eyes.

Miriam stepped closer and plucked the brush from Sundra's hand, wedging herself cleverly between the girl and her maid.

"Addie, go to Mrs. Reed and show her where the burial cerecloth is kept," commanded Miriam.

With Addie out of her way Miriam fell into silence as she gently pulled apart the snarls in Sundra's hair. She slowly brushed the locks until her repeated strokes brought back the rich luster of highlights.

While Miriam charaded as a hairdresser she kept fighting the urge to scream out her anger at Giles for jeopardizing her plans by dying at such an inconvenient time. Sundra was sure to balk, but no matter, thought Miriam. There were other ways to skin a cat.

"Miriam, since we've begun a year's time of mourning, do you suppose Elliot will pay for Father's debts, until we can marry next year on St. Ives day?" plyed Sundra with a false statement, trying to gain an insight into Miriam's thoughts now that her plans had unknowingly been exposed.

"La, you're such a naïve child. There's been no change in plans, my dear, for a number of reasons," replied Miriam, trying not to sound sarcastic. "First, it was your father's wish to have you married off. 'Tis written in the betrothal contract to forgo a proper time of mourning if it became necessary. If that isn't enough, the baronet's mother disinherited him when he agreed to marry you instead of her friend's daughter she had chosen for him. Dear Elliot hasn't a shilling to spare until you become his wife."

"And if I refuse?"

"You will regret it! According to the law, you and I will be held responsible for paying off the Bradford debts. Take heed, Sundra! Tyburn Prison is the place we'll be heading for. Imagine wearing filthy rags, sleeping on a dank floor crawling with vermin and fighting off the rats for rotten slime they call food! But, if that is your decision," sighed Miriam gloomily. "I won't deny I would have liked to have shared the dowry. My poor Giles. I don't think he really cared about the debts as much as he did for the foundling home. Those little children will surely suffer when they are turned out into the cold. Tsk, tsk, 'tis a shame!"

"Thrown out? You are not suggesting the Wellses would ever do such a thing! But why? What does my father's debts have to do with them?"

"Why, Sundra! Didn't you know it was Giles's money that kept up the foundling home? He'd been rewarding them through an endowment for giving you their love and kindness during the past years."

Sundra was facing a new dilemma. She thought Miriam had wanted the money only for herself. Yet, she couldn't believe her ears when Miriam pleaded for the sake of the orphans. She had no reason to lie, knowing the bulk of the inheritance would go directly into the vicarage fund. Other than being out of debt, Miriam would have nothing else to gain. Perhaps a meager sum to buy the bare necessities. No comforts. Not even an extra guinea would she have to toss on a gaming table!

"There must be a way for the Wellses to retain the endowment. I'll wager Sir Edmund Dillingham made some sort of stipulation when he wrote the contract," said Sundra, stalling for time to clear her thoughts.

"Oh, Sir Edmund is too old and senile to have handled the legalities," replied Miriam sympathetically. "Mr. Adrian Shaw drew up the documents. If you wish, I will send for him and we can go over the papers together. You may see for yourself that the contract is in perfect order."

Sundra did not reply, giving Miriam a chance to catch her breath.

"Sundra, do you love the Wellses enough to marry as scheduled so that the foundling home can continue saving helpless children? Their only chance of survival is resting upon your shoulders. No wedding . . . no money."

Sundra could never deny the love ingrained in her heart for the Wellses and the children. She was blind, and had no idea if her sight would ever return. How could she pass up this opportunity if it might be the last hope her future had in store for her.

And Elliot? Would living with him be a nightmare in itself? Or would he neglect a blind wife to seek pleasure in another woman's arms? Miriam's loving embraces! It could be a blessing in disguise; a shameful wish Sundra quickly put from her mind. "Do away with her permanently" jarred her memory. Could her father's death make a difference as to whether she stayed alive or not?

Miriam jumped to the conclusion that Sundra's mute state was a sign of surrender. She placed the brush on the dresser, pretending she laid down a winning hand of cards. She was going back to the gaming hells on St. James's Street after all! With a hidden smile of triumph she walked away from Sundra.

"You will make the most beautiful bride," whispered Miriam, strolling out of the room.

CHAPTER 4

Heavy drops of freezing rain pelted the scanty group of mourners paying their last respects to Lord Giles. Warily they touched his pine coffin with shivering hands, hesitating to linger in the tattered shroud of fog creeping past the thin rusted iron palisade of the secluded family plot. Billows of frozen breath followed the persons retracing their indented footprints in the sod. Uppermost in mind was to seek the warmth inside Bradtree Manor.

Sundra remained behind in the soggy field with Addie and Smitty flanked by her side. They joined hands and shared a private moment, allowing the others to drift away in a motley procession. Sundra was then smuggled without notice to the safety and privacy of her chambers.

A handful of inquisitive neighbors and villagers, the new minister from Chelsea, and the baroness were clustered around mahogany tables sipping tea and ratafia with their luncheon. They sampled the viands of roast leg of mutton, boiled fowl stuffed with dry oysters, parsley sauce and minced pies of beef at random. The frazzled serving maid, under Mrs. Reed's dictation, darted back and forth to the kitchen to replenish the Spode plates with apple tarts, Shrewsbury and seed cakes dribbled with quince preserves, rice custard and winter squash pudding.

The adjoining study was occupied by country squires with Sir Elliot acting as host. Sir Edmund mingled wherever a fresh tray of liquid refreshments was served. The men drank brandy and port from never empty glasses while they discussed the war with France at great length. Bets were wagered on the exact date when fickle spring would arrive to thaw England's countryside. Eventually they toasted Lord Giles. "Gone but not forgotten," they hypocritically proclaimed, having come to the wake merely out of curiosity over the charming young widow.

"Damn it all! What could be keeping Smitty," rasped Sir Elliot, loud enough to gain the barrister's attention. "I sent for some hot rum toddies to brace these fine gents against this wretched weather before they take their leave. Oh," he whined impatiently, "where is that old foozle!"

"Jolly good of you, ol' chap," slurred Sir Edmund. He welcomed the idea of another drink to help drown his sorrow. He went in search of the valet to hurry him along.

"Psst!"

Sir Edmund halted near the shadows of the back staircase, afraid to move away from the hulk walking toward him. Addie had found whom she was looking for but was not pleased with his condition. She mumbled in his ear and he followed her, tripping only once on the steps. He leaned heavily against Addie while she gave him a sketchy account of Sundra's misfortunes which led to her blindness.

Hoping that her shocking news had somehow cleared his foggy condition, Addie led the barrister into Sundra's room. Anxiously she checked the corridors to make certain no one had followed them upstairs to eavesdrop.

Sundra heard Sir Edmund sink wearily into the chair in front of her. The odor of brandy and cigar smoke assailed her nostrils. Her pounding heart skipped a beat.

"Oh, Sir Edmund! You can't imagine the shock of finding Elliot and Miriam in the garden," she told him dolefully, her voice quivering with a trace of bitterness. "I'm convinced Father's heart failed because he witnessed their cozy tryst from his window. I had fallen and hit my head and, by the time I found my way back to the manor, Father was dead."

"Damnation," roared the barrister, puffing and coughing to clear his throat. His fuddled mind was ranting and raving, yet his lips remained sealed with disgust. He swayed in his seat, suddenly finding it difficult to keep open his drooping eyelids. Beads of perspiration trickled down his wrinkled temples.

"Those two heathens robbed his lordship of his life!" Addie spoke up harshly, unable to resist butting into the conversation. She poked the barrister's shoulder with her elbow. When he looked up at her, startled, Addie merely pointed her finger at Sundra, motioning for him to take a good look. "My Sunny has lost her eyesight, but they'll never know what trouble they've caused her. No, sir! 'Tis why you're here," she said, sharply nudging him once more.

"Here now," grunted Sir Edmund. "Miss Sundra, please! This is all very confusing. What's going on here?" he demanded to know, somewhat relieved that Addie was now perched near the doorway where she couldn't take another jab at him.

"I must escape from Bradtree before Miriam and Elliot learn that I discovered their secret. My life depends on it," she confessed, and took a deep breath to help steady her nerves. "I must be frank, kind sir, and come to the point. I ask that you loan me two thousand pounds."

Sundra heard the barrister shuffling his feet. Her request was met by an ominous silence. "I want to go back to the foundling home," she hurried to say, explaining she didn't want to be a burden. Also, the loan would supplement the Wellses financially until someone of greater means granted them an endowment.

Sir Edmund's mind was groggy and wandered into oblivion. He conjured Sundra's likeness into a newborn lamb about to be thrown to a pack of hungry wolves. The thought chilled him to the bone.

"I may be blind, but I've seen flashes of light. Oh, Sir Edmund," she whispered with emotion, "one day I may be able to see again!"

Sundra's voice was a weak echo which scarcely penetrated his thoughts on the brunt of the tragedy.

"Sir Edmund! Haven't you been listening?" cried Sundra.

"What? Oh yes, child. You are sorely incapacitated," he whined absentmindedly. "Poor girl . . ."

Sundra was in a dither over the barrister's melancholy stupor. "I haven't a future unless you can help me," she pleaded.

The barrister's head was spinning. He wished Sundra had talked more slowly and less excitedly into his feeble ears.

Of course, he thought to himself, Giles's daughter had a right to be upset. She just told him she had no future, which brought only one conclusion to his numbed brain—the poor girl did not have long to live!

Sir Edmund went to Sundra to give her a sympathetic hug, tripped on the carpet and grabbed the draperies to keep from sprawling into her lap. He paused and tried to clear his mind, to sober his thoughts and speech.

"The wool's been pulled over my eyes," he conceded. "Lady Miriam came to my office a month ago and told me a cock-and-bull story about Giles squandering his fortune. Mind you, I had no reason to doubt her word at the time."

Egad! He felt those miserable blotches spreading down the scruff of his neck. He wiped his brow, his cheeks and chin, paying more attention to refolding his handkerchief than was necessary; anything to avoid looking at Sundra's pitiful face. "I gave her every guinea I owned, just so I could be of help to my dear friend Giles," he sniffed, his eyes misting with tears over the memories of a departed crony. "I'm as poor as a churchmouse unless my funds are repaid."

"But Miriam thinks I am going to marry Elliot! I beg of you, please don't let that happen to me!"

"The devil take me! I'm too old to even offer you my protection. I wish I were in the grave instead of your dear father." Sir Edmund tapped his teeth with his knuckles. He felt useless. Despondent. "Dearest Sundra, forgive me," he croaked. He stumbled, then quickly ran out of the room so Sundra and Addie couldn't hear him bawling.

Sir Edmund scuttled beneath the pouring rain, his boots plunking through swollen puddles littering the courtyard until he found his horse and carriage. He slumped in the driver's seat; his aching head wouldn't allow him to sit straight.

"Giddap, Pete. I've had enough. Go on, git!" he babbled, giving the horse a slack rein to lead on. The buggy swayed as he drove down the winding lane through spitting rain and dreary patches of fog.

"You take us over to the Black Douglas Inn," yawned Sir Edmund, nestled against the canvas hood. "Mind that you don't stop along the way," he told the horse. Finally he allowed his eyes to close, feeling confident that the sight of Pete's bobbing rump and prancing legs would eventually take him to his destination.

The Black Douglas Inn was teeming with raucous laughter and thirsty laborers waiting for the paymaster who had told them to come here. As the hour wore thin, the men turned to spending wages they had yet to receive. The paymaster was always tardy, yet quick enough to sneak behind the taproom and receive his share of the extra profits from the proprietor, with no one else the wiser.

"C'mon, Tubbins! Give us a free sampling o' tha foin rum I heard ye got stashed away fer the gentry," demanded the blacksmith, winking in drunken jest at the proprietor. " 'Tis tha least ye kin do fer sittin' our cold arses by the blasted door!" His eyes wandered across the smoke-filled, cavernous room to gaze with a longing at the fieldstone hearth where the fire consumed wide tree stumps instead of spindled logs.

"If I know the likes of you, Roscoe, 'tis not the drink, nor the fire, but Coralee you be awantin'," laughed Tubbins. He grinned a toothless smile from ear to ear. His business was good at the inn on paydays, but fared even better whenever his comely niece helped out. Tubbins payed special attention to the blacksmith's craving for Coralee. Roscoe wasn't the first to ask for her, which set his mind to thinking. He could get a handsome price from the Quality if she was willing to be a good sport, which she wasn't. He'd see about that! Tubbins wiped his hand down the front of his stained apron and tapped another hogshead of ale to keep up with the thirsty demands of a ribald crowd.

A draft of cold air blasted the villagers seated near the entrance when Gardner Foxworthy, the Duke of Trentbay, pushed his way inside.

"Well now, wot ye look who's 'ere," whispered a man sitting next to the blacksmith.

"Aye, 'tis tha devil hisself," claimed Roscoe, wiping froth from his lips with his soiled shirt sleeve.

The men's annoyed glances were quickly tamed by Gardner's look of rage as he surveyed the room with piercing eyes, his muscles taut and flexed, ready to do battle with anyone standing in his way.

"Tubbins," boomed Gardner's voice, "where is Sir James Moore?"

"Sir James is in tha gamin' room, Your Grace." Tubbins pointed toward the narrow hallway leading to the private room in the rear of the inn. He asked his lordship if he'd like a bottle of his best brandy sent to his table. The duke brushed past Tubbins without giving him a second thought.

"Your turn, Adrian," said James as he sat back in his chair and tilted backward, showing his boredom by untying his neck stock and yawning loudly. James didn't mind playing a few rounds of faro with the lawyer while he waited for Gardner, but he did object to gambling with a poor player, especially when the young dandy forced his companionship on him in the first place.

James waited for Adrian to place his bet on the table before turning up the top card of the deck.

"If you would pay more attention to playing cards instead of asking so many questions about Gardner, we'd be done by now," James badgered him. "Lud! I'd swear you already knew the duke would be late just by the way you carry on."

Adrian Shaw felt he had dallied long enough. He tossed the last of his guineas on the green felt, making sure he carefully replaced the fold over his breast pocket.

"No need to be vexed with me, Sir James," pouted Adrian,

flicking off a minuscule piece of cigar ash from his lapel. "I rarely get the chance to practice my skills on cards. The court keeps me tied down with paperwork. But, today has been quite a pleasure," Adrian admitted gleefully, "even if my pockets are let."

Inwardly, Adrian was disappointed that he didn't have the necessary stakes to stay in the game to dig for more information about the duke, yet pleased he knew why His Grace would be late, if he showed up at all.

Shaw was ready to take his leave with a bow. Suddenly two hands grabbed his shoulders and spun him around with a savage force. A powerful fist connected squarely on his jaw and sent him crashing through the tables and chairs like a bull running in a china shop.

Gardner attacked Adrian again, pinning him against the wall with ease. He seized the lawyer's throat with a steel grip and forced him to look up into his penetrating eyes blazing with anger.

"What's happened to Alice?" demanded Gardner. "Tell me quick, or I'll choke the truth out of you right here and now!"

James shoved his way across the room that was beginning to fill with drunken onlookers. It was obvious Adrian couldn't utter a sound by the way Gardner was squeezing his neck.

"Damn it, Gardner," yelled James. "Ease up on the poor bastard. What in hell is going on here?"

Everyone in the room hushed each other so they could hear better. The duke relaxed his hold. Adrian coughed and gasped for breath.

"I don't know what you're talking about," sputtered the lawyer. "See here! You've smutched my coat." In a split-second decision Adrian suddenly twisted his body and broke free. He shouted to the crowd: "He's a madman!" and tried to make a run for the door.

Gardner lunged forward and threw him to the floor. A tiny piece of gold tumbled out of Adrian's pocket and rolled toward the throng. He scrambled on all fours, trying to put as much distance as possible between himself and the duke.

All hell broke loose the instant Gardner recognized the gold piece as his sister's ring. He unleashed his fury and charged after the fleeing lawyer like a devil bounding after a blackened soul.

Shouts and curses sprang up from the excited crowd. Gardner's wrath had stirred the men into a disorderly fracas. Arms and fists were swinging freely, bodies clashed in every direction. The laborers reveled in their passion for a drunken brawl, never mind the motive.

While most of the mob remained inside to grapple, Gardner and Adrian tumbled out into the livery courtyard to skirmish beyond the skeptical taunters.

"Pray, leave me be," sobbed Adrian. "I never meant to hurt her . . . I'll tell you everything."

Gardner stood with his boots planted firmly in the mud, ready to charge, but remained stationary when the lawyer appealed for mercy. He gave Adrian a chance to have his say, for he wasn't getting any nearer the truth by bashing the man.

"If you want information about Alice," remarked Adrian, suddenly changing his surrendering tone into a sneer, putting as much emphasis on the girl's name as possible, "then you better take warning. Don't you dare raise your fist to me again, or the next time I see your sister, she'll not be so lucky."

The duke sported a scoffing smile at Adrian's comment. "Don't tell me that a cowardly fool such as yourself would dare to lay a hand on my sister," sneered Gardner.

"No, my job was to see that she sailed without you, for which I received her gold ring as payment. I don't know how you knew I was involved, but at this point, I don't much care. I'm going to enjoy watching your high-and-mighty empire come crashing down on you. 'Tis starting already," he said arrogantly. "Wouldn't you like to know who in your confidential circle of friends betrayed you?"

Adrian withdrew his gloves and rubbed his cold fingers together as he strutted over to the silent duke. "Not to worry! I'm certain you'll find money somewhere to put bread in your family's mouth," chuckled Adrian. "What's this! Is his lordship speechless?"

Adrian stuck his long pointed nose high up in the air and, being in a certain mood to display his twisted sense of amusement, slapped his soiled gloves across the duke's face to harass him; to wallow in his momentary glory of being the battle's victor. But as his hand delivered the insult Roscoe had staggered from the inn and, seeing what looked to him like the preliminaries of a gentlemen's fight of honor, yelled "Duel" for all to hear.

Adrian wore a stunned expression on his palled face. You bloomin' idiot, he thought in nervous dismay, 'tis not what I meant at all! His scrawny legs took giant steps in the muck to move a safe distance away from Gardner. Cautiously, he looked over his shoulder, fearing an uprising. Gardner was just as surprised at the blacksmith's assumption as Adrian was.

By now the rowdies were jamming the doorway. The frigid shower of rain didn't quench their thirst for cold blood as they continued in a frenzy to get outside. James was caught in the pack's middle and was frantically trying to throw leveling punches to clear a path in order to reach Gardner.

"I am more than willing to oblige your challenge, Shaw. I've the privilege of choosing which weapons we're to use, am I not right?" Gardner remarked craftily.

"No! 'Twas a jest, sir. Nothing more," stammered Adrian. "I don't want to fight you. All I ever wanted was your mon—"

"My money! What makes you so certain you'll receive a shilling from my coffers? A blackguard's promise? Tell me who struck a deal with you, and why," asked Gardner, watching the shadow of doubt creep across Adrian's miserly face. He knew the coward wouldn't be able to hold his tongue much longer. "Who's your second, for we'll touch swords!"

"No!" shouted Adrian. "I don't want to die!"

"Why was I detained at dockside," demanded Gardner harshly. "And who's responsible for letting you be privy to my confidential accounts? If you value your life, then speak up!"

As Adrian continued to look exceedingly worried, he noticed someone moving in the bushes behind the duke's back. "M-m-my informant is . . ." claimed Adrian, his last word barely a desperate whisper. His mouth dropped open. His right hand reached inside his coat pocket. Very slowly, he withdrew a pistol and pointed it at Gardner.

Unaware that the lawyer's eyes were focused on the bushes next to him, Gardner quickly reacted by dropping to the ground. He looked at Adrian standing idle, then caught sight of branches rustling alongside of where he was laying.

A black-gloved hand emerged from the thicket and, pointing a pistol at Adrian, shot him in cold blood.

Adrian staggered backward, his muscles twitching in pain. The heavy veil of death was covering him, but he struggled under the pressure to get in the last shot. His firearm exploded as he gurgled his last breath.

The shot meant for Adrian's attacker went astray and imbedded itself in Gardner's shoulder. The impact threw him against the hitching post. Stunned and unable to move, Gardner could only watch as the unknown assailant threw down the weapon at his feet before running off into the woods.

Boisterous shouting mixed with rebellious cries filled the air. Gardner knew he was being accused of dueling by the mob's reaction. The King's law had been broken, which meant the officials would soon be poking their noses in everybody's business during a thorough investigation. Since most of the men were probably smugglers, Gardner knew his chances of getting out of this situation were slim. The locals would either deliver him to the law, which would seriously hamper his plans to leave England, or they would hush the scandal by getting rid of the evidence, including himself.

Occupied with settling individual differences, the crowd didn't rush to imprison the wounded offender because he was in no condition to run off. Gardner called for James while he tried his best to staunch the bleeding. The last thing he saw was a horse and carriage speeding down the road toward the inn.

"Hell and damnation," cursed Sir Edmund as he fought to keep his horse under control. The carriage wheels jammed and sent a thick spray of muddied water up into the air. The buggy slid past the bend and veered off the road into the midst of clamor. Sir Edmund kicked the brake handle into a locked position with his boot, none too pleased at being rudely awakened, nearly wrenched from his seat, and having ruined a good pair of leathers within a matter of minutes. The underside of his carriage was amass with ceaselessly dripping brown rivulets.

"What the deuce," he heaved as he jumped precariously to the ground. He saw a horde of riffraff milling around a corpse in the mud. He gasped in dismay when he recognized the body of Adrian Shaw, an unscrupulous member of the court's staff. Sir Edmund was mortified and cried out, "A scandalous effusion of the blood," to no one in particular. He clucked his tongue, feeling no compassion for Shaw or the other belligerents obstructing his path.

"He's innocent! Someone else fired the gun," shouted the burly-looking man filled with an angry rage as he stood sentinel over his wounded companion. The man turned and grabbed Sir Edmund's arm as he tried to pass them on his way to observe the corpse.

"Dillingham! Give me a hand."

"Here now," scolded Sir Edmund, trying to wrench free. "Let go or I'll . . . uhh, Sir James!" he exclaimed, taken unaware by an acquaintance he held in high esteem. "Dear lud!" Sir Edmund nearly fainted when he glanced downward and saw Gardner Foxworthy trying to stand up, a crimson stain spreading across his shoulder which branded him a participator in what the barrister had surmised as a dastardly deed before he knew the duke was involved.

"Justifiable," announced Sir Edmund, without benefit of the facts, for a Foxworthy could do no wrong in his eyes. The barrister sucked in a deep breath, about to launch into an oration to absolve Gardner of wrongdoing.

James cast a worried look at the gathering crowd, a lynching mob no doubt, and wasn't about to stand around to ponder the issues with the benevolent old windbag.

"Your home is not far off, Dilly. Take us there," commanded James, "and do hurry!"

Sir Edmund whipped his horse into a lather as they escaped

along the highway like madmen, bracing themselves as their coach went lurching around the corner at the crossroads.

"For the life of me, I can't imagine how Adrian came to possess your sister's ring," yelled Sir Edmund. "Are you positive it was hers?"

"Yes," growled Gardner. He had not been mistaken. His parents had bequeathed their identical wedding rings to him. He showed Sir Edmund the crested ring on his finger. "Since I have yet to find a lady worthy of bearing my name, I gave it to Alice. A gift of sentiment, from one who's heart she coyly compared to the cold hollow of a dripping cave. She is with child."

"I tried to keep the rowdies under control while Gardner was trying to get the truth out of Shaw," added James. "The next thing I knew, Gardner and Adrian were grappling outside and someone fired from the bushes. Every drunken lout misunderstood the scene completely during the fracas and started to blame Gardner for dueling while he lay wounded from Adrian's stray shot."

Although he had admitted being in league with a rough lot from the waterfront and that he was somehow privy to the duke's financial problems, Adrian had been deliberately murdered before he could utter the truth.

Old Pete's nostrils were flared from exhaustion, sending a stream of heated breath into the nipping air. His sides were heaving, and he lathered at the flanks as he obediently cantered along the isolated street leading to his master's stable.

Having left the duke in James's care in the upper guest room, Sir Edmund made a place for himself in the kitchen alcove. He sat haphazardly on a ladderback chair. Every joint in his body felt stiff. His head reeled as he pondered the day's complications.

The duke and he had the same basic problem—no money! Gardner's fortune was questionably tied up in his Canadian estate and lumber company, but his was lost forever because of Lady Miriam's deceit. He owed a long-standing debt to the Foxworthy family, and now that Gardner could use his financial help, Sir Edmund was totally useless.

At this point no one would willingly loan money to the duke, thought Sir Edmund. By daybreak all the gossiping wags in London would falsely accuse Gardner of dueling. No decent Englishman would risk the King breathing down his neck if he aided a lawbreaker, Quality or not!

Sir Edmund was occupied in thought while he was pouring boiling water into a teapot. The rising steam from the copper kettle quickly burned his hand.

"Blasted women's work," he grumbled, soundly cursing the caldron. While rummaging the sideboard for a slab of butter, he thought it was a pity that Addie wasn't around to soothe his burn by rubbing her special salve on it. An unexpected idea struck his fancy as he was spooning tea leaves into a silver strainer.

"Drink for thought!" Exalted, Sir Edmund took a huge swallow from a decanter of rum. He smacked his lips in appreciation and swiftly gulped down another jiggerful. With a large goblet in hand he prepared to imbibe to his heart's content. He'd take the tea upstairs—much later!

Gardner was comfortably braced against the headboard after drinking a mug of rum. James cut his silk shirt and exposed a patch of curly black hair which covered the tanned and muscular mounds of his chest. After the wad of gauze was removed, a thin stream of blood trickled from the swollen hole. James splashed rum on the wound with his left hand while his other hand fumbled with a steel probe as he tried to dig out the lead ball. He worked the instrument back and forth until he felt a dull grating within the flesh as the two metals came into contact.

Gardner's face was beginning to show signs of strain and perspiration, yet he did not complain when the coarse probe penetrated deeper into his bruised muscle. James drained a mouthful of liquor to steady his nerves. His arms were straining by the time he dislodged the bullet. The duke gave him a nod of gratitude.

"Damn it, Gardner! You make me feel like a bloody surgeon," James said, breathing a sigh of relief. He studied the duke's face, the same rugged but handsome face that made women desire his attentions, sycophants and heiresses alike. "Next you'll be telling me an Indian maiden taught you how not to flinch, or is that vice versa?" He placed the slug on the nightstand and covered the wound with a clean bandage, placing Gardner's arm in a cloth restraint.

"Living in Canada has its rewards," smiled Gardner, his expression suddenly turning serious. "If it wasn't for Alice, I would never have left. Now step aside, I have to get back to the *Northwind* to make sure all is in order before we sail."

"What! And start bleeding all over again? You can at least wait until Dilly brings up a tray."

"I have no idea if Alice will arrive in Canada dead or alive," shouted Gardner aggressively. "Don't play nursemaid with me, old friend," he growled, "nor take advantage of our fellowship. The *Northwind* will sail with or without you!"

Gardner's eyes turned cold and calculating, barely able to restrain his flaring temper. Defiantly he untied the sling cradling his left arm and threw it away.

"I don't believe this!" spouted James, throwing up his arms. "You'd have heard by now if your sister came to any harm. Why break your neck to go sailing back home, when you can stay to investigate your financial discrepancy?"

"Because I'm responsible for her welfare!"

The muscles in Gardner's cheek twitched in spasms of fury, his fists tightly clenched by his side. "Why I let Charles persuade me to fetch Alice, I'll never know." He was thoroughly irritated with himself as well. "He should have taken her back to Canada three months ago when he was on leave and had visited with her in England."

Still, Gardner had to admit that coming back to England also gave him the opportunity to hire men to work his tobacco fields. And there was Alice Rose Hawthorne, delighted to welcome him back with an ultimatum; remain with her in London or sever their relationship so someone else could appreciate her favors. A shopping jaunt was all it took to placate her injured pride, because Gardner refused to be cajoled, putting an end to their stormy liaison.

"The outskirts of an uncompleted military post three months ago was not an ideal place to house a woman, least of all a wife," reasoned James. "Besides, the Hewett homestead has just been completed. Now that the couple is expecting a child, you can't blame them for wanting to be together."

Gardner's sensation of guilt was adding fuel to his fiery rage. If he hadn't been called to recheck the bill of lading, Alice wouldn't have been left unattended at the dockside while anticipating a voyage to her new homeland. And she being in such a delicate condition! How could he have been so negligent?

"When you return home without a penny in your pocket and see that Alice is happily knitting little mitts of linen, you will regret not heeding my advice to put your ledgers in order," cautioned James sarcastically.

Sir Edmund snickered when he overheard his guests shouting. He entered the room with a smile on his face, his mind silently mulling over the words which he must carefully choose for his strategic proposal.

The barrister poured tea heavily laced with rum into pewter mugs and waited for the hearty aroma to fill the air. With self-assured dignity he cleared his throat and unrolled a parchment displaying his bold handwriting.

"Gentlemen, feast your eyes on this!" he proclaimed in a nasal tone of authority, similar to the way he addressed the courts. "Within this cornucopian writ," he boasted, "is the perfect solution to our bloody problems!"

The chilled deluge which plagued the countryside had finally subsided. It was pitch black outside tonight, on the eve of St. Ives, and the air was being warmed by sudden gusts of wind.

Branches of a linden tree scratched and tapped narrow wooden fingers against the chapel window panes at Bradtree. Invisible drafts, escaping from the darkness, seeped through numerous cracks to refresh the stale air inside the stone-built room where Sundra and Addie awaited the night's outcome on tenterhooks.

"Why the worried frown on your face?" asked Addie, wondering why tonight, of all nights, Sundra had to look so panic-stricken. Carefully she adjusted a flounce and stood back to admire the muslin wedding gown on Sundra. "I thought Sir Edmund did away with your doubting Thomas attitude."

"He was practically in his cups, Addie! He promised that I would become the wife of Gardner Foxworthy, the Duke of Trentbay. It's hard to believe Sir Edmund could have arranged such a match! Oh, look how late it is," she exclaimed nervously. "Sir Edmund probably never intended to show his face here again, much less bring a bridegroom with him."

"Sir Edmund arranged to have Lady Miriam called away, and she's gone for the night, isn't she? And he promised that Mrs. Reed wouldn't be back from Chelsea before . . . now, see here, young lady," clucked Addie, "who're you tryin' to fool? Miss Sunny, if you've filled your head with those romantic notions again, I'll . . ."

Addie's warning was cut short because Sundra's expression confirmed her suspicion. "Oh, Sundra, how could you," she said in exasperation.

"Doesn't every girl wish for love on her wedding day? Isn't it heartbreaking enough that I don't feel like a bride-to-be, that I can't allow myself the privilege because I'm a hypocrite! I agreed to an immediate annulment. How do you think I feel to go against what Reverend Wells had taught me about obeying the laws of the church!"

"Poppycock," hissed Addie, taking hold of Sundra's shoulders, ready to shake sense into her on the spot. Addie questioned Sundra's motives. Would Sundra have wed Sir Elliot even though he and his harlot plotted against her, just because she felt obligated by some rules?

Sundra didn't know what to expect out of life anymore. She had a chance to escape her stepmother's treachery by marrying the duke, a stranger who surely didn't love her. Yet, she forgot about common sense, never caring why the duke was complying with the barrister's scheme, and let her heart be captured by the gallantry of her would-be rescuer. She didn't know if she was confusing affection with gratitude. As long as she had the

Foxworthy name to protect her, she didn't care. Somehow Sundra managed to include the duke in her daydreams. Strange as it seems, the thought comforted her.

"If only we could benefit from the legalities without abusing the church laws. The vows are sacred, and I wish . . ."

"Wishing again!" snorted Addie in dismay. "Your marriage will be in name only, missy. Within an hours time you'll meet this gallant duke of whatever, and then part to go your separate ways. Believe me," warned the maid with a husky retort, "as much as you'd like to think he's Prince Charming, he's got his own God Almighty reasons for giving up his bachelorhood so easily. Humph! He's anxious all right, to get this whole affair over and done with. Otherwise ol' Dilly would be bringing His Grace to the altar by the seat of his breeches!"

Sundra held back her tears. She had to admit that as a blind woman she shouldn't expect to have a loving husband and a houseful of children. What man in his right mind would have her? The truth hurt. Perhaps this was why she felt it wasn't wrong to allow her heart to race like wildfire just for the moment; to help forget the depressing hours of being drilled that her tender emotions should never surface during the wedding ceremony.

Addie gave Sundra a reassuring hug and patted her gently on the back. They waited for the minutes to tick past the midnight hour to bring St. Ives's day into existence.

"Coo, child," soothed Addie. "A man who's willing to give you up is not worth crying for. Makes a body wonder where His Grace received his upbringing. None the less," she added quickly, "'tis what's been agreed upon. Save those wishes for another time, and don't waste them on some pompous coward." Addie folded her mistress' pelisse over her arm and shuffled across the slate floor heading toward the vestry.

The wall sconces cast an ivory sheen on Sundra as she stood by the oak railing which led to the pulpit. Her hair was styled in flowing curls, resting softly upon her shoulders much like the gentle swells of full-bodied waves covering a breaker alongside the harbor. The embroidery of lace accented the creamy whiteness of her skin. Wisps of smoke from burning beeswax candles breezed past her still figure and subtly blended with her scent of lily-of-the-valley.

"I'd give a bald-headed monkey a kiss on his noggin'," chortled Addie, "to see the look on Lady Miriam's face when she learns you've succeeded without her meddling and that you are not to be found."

Addie's quip brought a sad smile to Sundra's lips. Yes, she felt lucky indeed to be leaving Bradtree, for it was no longer a vestige of hearthside to her without her father.

The chapel door's rusted hinges squeaked when a small gathering of gentlemen entered the church. It was midnight.

The men filed past the aged archway. Addie was eased aside to the wall and, since she couldn't immediately return to Sundra's side, bided her time by observing the proceedings. The minister and Sir Edmund were donning spectacles to view the documents to make sure all was in order. The best man was Sir James Moore, who stood transfixed near the marble column and stared at the lovely bride-to-be.

"Looks to me they're dressed for a wake," fancied the pessimistic maid. And the duke? Strange that she should miss "his" entrance!

Out of the corner of her eye, Addie caught sight of a sudden movement in the far corner of the room. A tall gentleman was emerging from the darkened vestry. He was wearing a well-cut suit of black velvet, and his shirt and stock were fashioned from the finest white silk Addie had ever seen. Her eyes widened at his presence; a look of awe. He was more imposing in stature than any other man in the chamber.

The gentlemen greeted him with a bow and called him "Your Grace," in their salutations. Addie's heart skipped a beat as she flattened her backside against the wall. "O Lord have mercy," she whispered through gritted teeth. Could the duke have entered without her notice or had he been standing in the vestry all along, overhearing her sour comments whether he wanted to or not? Addie couldn't determine if he was scowling, because his face remained hidden in the shadows.

"Lady Sundra!" hailed Sir Edmund as he hurried to enter the chamber ahead of the others. "You look ravishing, child, simply ravishing!" He whispered his approval in her ear and added, "I've brought none other than the duke's family minister!" Sir Edmund was chortling with satisfaction at how well his plans were working out.

Sundra was not impressed. She felt more guilty than ever. The thought of being bound to a man she didn't know nor could not see was traumatic enough, but to deceive a high-standing man of the cloth by promising to cherish and obey her vows when she had agreed to annul it afterward was making her conscience suffer. Sundra felt a pang of pity for the duke, thinking it wasn't easy for him either to withhold the clause from his minister.

Sundra trembled. When she heard the gentlemen approaching in her direction, she prepared to follow Addie's advice. "It will look best," Addie had hinted, "if you don't appear to look afflicted, especially at your own wedding. Be brave, raise that proud chin, and show them that you are every bit the lady of quality that you are."

Sundra listened to the introductions and acknowledged their good wishes with dignity. She didn't need their pity over her blindness, nor did she perceive it in their conversation because her instincts accepted their sincerity.

The duke stood apart from the small group fussing over his bride-to-be. He never thought he'd ever see the little firebrand again. Shouldn't she be just as surprised as he was?

Gardner ignored the curious glances the maid was giving him. He stared straight ahead at Sundra, who had looked at him but had not shown any visible signs of recognizing him. The duke raised his eyebrow. He expected to receive another hate-filled glare from her; the same face she had given him on the day when he took Alice Rose Hawthorne on a shopping jaunt and had collided with her and the maid.

"Damn the sight of that girl for looking so winsome," thought Gardner. Any other time and she would have quickly stirred his passion with her innocent beauty, but he had Alice's welfare and fallible finances to think about and the problem weighed too heavily on his mind.

Gardner wanted Sundra to sneer her contempt at him. Perhaps he could be less critical of his actions knowing she didn't enjoy participating in this arrangement to gain her dowry any more than he did.

Thinking Sundra could not recognize him because of the murky shadows, the duke moved forward into the amber candlelight, baiting her to lose her composure. He heard a stifled gasp from the portly maid who was holding up the walls in the corner.

With a graceful stance and nodding in agreement during the flow of comments around her, Sundra casually moved her head and scanned with sightless green eyes the childhood memories of the vestibule where the duke was now standing.

Sundra's blank stare aroused Gardner's curiosity. Expressionless, he observed her from a distance, riveting his piercing eyes on her petite figure. It was obvious she held her audience captive by her demure charms rather than with a sympathetic hand-holding. Somehow Sir Edmund's story about Sundra being so desperately ill that she needed a portion of her dowry to make her last days on earth bearable did not ring true! Gardner thought Sundra looked in excellent health. Why did she appear timid and refuse to acknowledge that in London she had found him disgusting and not now? More puzzling was the fact Sundra acted as though she had never seen him before.

Then, an astonishing fact struck him. 'Twas a game of wit! Either she was out to snare him in marriage because he was in a vulnerable position or she was greedy for her money. A vixen turned pliant long enough to get what she wanted. The duke was satisfied the dowry was divided in his favor. A sardonic smile formed on his lips when he remembered the annulment papers in his possession.

Once again Gardner knew he would be the winner in this game of charades that females play. He had learned from past experiences to be wary of coy women who took an interest in him when all they ever wanted was his wealth, social position, and power. He had grown to detest conniving ladies, which was why he never had a binding relationship with one for very long.

Gardner moved forward with long strides and stood next to Sundra, towering over her and the men, who respectfully backed away to take their rightful positions by the altar to await His Lordship's command to start the ceremony.

"At last, 'tis a pleasure to make your proper acquaintance," claimed Gardner as he took hold of her hand and held it gently.

Sundra bowed her head and allowed her hand to remain in his control, feeling his warmth spreading across her skin to make her body tingle with nervous excitement.

"Am I forgiven of any past indiscretions so that I may be your humble servant, m'lady?" he spoke softly, concealing the sarcasm in his voice. Gardner felt her tremble, the corners of his mouth twisting into a mocking smile.

The stranger's voice belonged to a young gentleman, thought Sundra. His strong yet subdued tone suggested that she should not pass harsh judgment on him for being a willing partner in this mockery of a marriage. How noble of him to consider her feelings!

Sundra felt certain her father would have approved of the stranger's gallantry. The image of Lord Giles made Sundra smile without her being aware that her fond recollections were making her face glow from bittersweet memories.

Slowly, Gardner overturned Sundra's hand and leisurely placed an intimate kiss on her palm. Sundra was startled by his sudden gesture, because he had caught her unaware while she was daydreaming. Shamefaced that he might think she had encouraged his intentions, she wanted to correct the bold error by trying to remove her hand from his grasp.

The duke restrained her with ease, nearly crushing her useless hand against a long-stemmed rose. "Be still," he murmured, forcing her fingers to close around it. Oblivious to what the others were thinking, he allowed his anger to spread across his face when he pulled her embarrassingly close against his lean, hardened body. "Was the love in your smile for me, madam, or for the jingle of gold I can put in your pockets?" he taunted.

"If memory serves me correct, I've done nothing to change your opinion of me, so don't play me for the fool."

"Your Grace, please," Sundra's voice quivered, "you don't understand. I wasn't thinking . . . I mean . . ." She stopped stammering in order to compose herself, cringing at the thought of making a scene in the chapel. She never realized how much the duke objected to a marriage of convenience and decided to leave his injured pride well enough alone. "Please, let's not argue," she whispered softly.

Sundra was allowed to withdraw her hand—slowly. His crude and unjust remark had wiped the serenity from her face. She held the posy defensively close to her breast, uncertain why her heart still went out to the duke even though his verbal chastisement had more than marred her spirit.

"My pardon, Miss Bradford. If you are in such dire straits, then don't let your heart keep emotional secrets, nor pretend that this marriage is anything but a serious matter of necessity."

Amid Addie's constant sniffling, Gardner and Sundra repeated their vows at quarter past midnight. The duke placed his mother's gold-crested ring on Sundra's third finger and in return received Lord Giles's cameo ring from Sundra. The minister's proclamation that they were man and wife sounded hollow in the somber room.

Sundra didn't know what to expect as she waited for the traditional kiss from the bridegroom. In an outrageous way, she was eager to feel the duke's lips on hers; for in her kiss he would have no doubts that she was saying good-bye forever.

The duke placed a brotherly peck on Sundra's forehead and just as quickly led her off to sign the certificate that the witnesses had already validated.

Sundra was not only disappointed with Gardner's tepid kiss, she was humiliated to have been pulled along like a tottering child. She wasn't used to walking ahead at such a fast pace in her sightless condition. When she had hesitated, he merely tightened his grip and forced her to quicken her pace.

Gardner held Sundra's hand aloft and directed her toward Addie, who was holding open the silk pelisse for her mistress.

Sundra raced courageously ahead with fearless steps, bold and determined to get farther away from the duke, who obviously regarded her in disdain. She misjudged her bearing and bumped awkwardly into an archway column which stood next to the banister's spacious opening.

Addie was ready to collapse into a fit of the vapors. The duke's fast action to support Sundra, and a ferocious stare, kept the maid and everyone else from rushing to aide the embarrassed girl.

"For Christ's sake," the duke whispered harshly in her ear. "The least you can do is control yourself before you go rushing off to grab your share of the dowry! A few minutes ago I believed this occasion meant more to you than a business matter. Obviously, I was mistaken."

Sundra inhaled sharply. "Sir, you forget yourself! You've complied with this marriage of convenience just as much as I was forced into it for reasons of my own. Take your hands off me, you . . . you arrogant devil," warned Sundra, his laughter pricking her ears as she lunged past the flabbergasted maid and bolted out of the chapel.

Sundra felt the sting from Gardner's false accusation as she clung to the churchyard's picket fence. How foolish she was to have wished for a simple endearment to help ease the pain of a loveless marriage, vowing she would never put herself in this position again. All she wanted to do now was to resume her life in the country and hoped that in time she would forget.

The gentlemen, silent and politely feigning ignorance of the bride's calamity, buttoned their great coats against the wind as they left the chapel, retreating under a cover of darkness.

The duke was anxious to proceed and shouted orders to his driver who was helping load the maid's trunk onto the barrister's coach. Gardner watched the wind whipping the froth of lace on Sundra's dress while she was standing alone by the fence. Her forlorn expression didn't fool him one bit. Whether she knew it or not, beneath her aura of ice-cold purity she was an emotional firebrand. There was something about Sundra which kept drawing Gardner's attention, holding him intrigued.

She was a rare one, he thought, chuckling at her brief display of hot-blooded temper. No one, least of all a girl, had ever dared to call him an arrogant devil. "Damn it," he thought excitedly. It would be a challenge to tame her before the pitfalls of greed spoiled her rotten!

Sundra was desperately trying to calm herself, knowing the moment was near to venture forth in life without Addie by her side. She hoped Sir Edmund knew what a wonderful woman he was getting with Addie as his new housekeeper. It was going to be very difficult to say good-bye.

Sundra nearly jumped when she heard the crunch of Addie's heavy footsteps approaching her.

"You've a right to give me a I-told-you-so lecture, Addie, but not now . . . please," said Sundra, sighing softly. "I was a fool to think I would be treated differently on my wedding day. It's a wonder His Grace didn't throw the lot of us out! Imagine, he even gave me a . . . a peck of gratitude," she said indignantly. "And to think I wanted to send him off with a good-bye kiss he'd never forget? Ha! . . . Addie? Is something wrong?" she asked, worried that the maid's silence was a warning in itself.

Gardner gripped Sundra's shoulders and spun her around to face him. His arms encircled her while he backed her up against a tree and urgently pressed his body close to hers. The duke captured her lips before she could cry out, taking her breath away with a prolonged, impetuous kiss.

Sundra struggled to escape from his embrace, to free herself of the pressure and warmth from his body which was causing her heart to beat wildly. His kiss was intense against her tremulous lips, yet she couldn't help but feel a strange, bewitching, sensation threatening to overpower her senses.

Sundra's knees were shaking by the time Gardner released her. She steadied herself, imagining a wicked smile on his face, that his legs were standing firmly apart.

"Have I remedied your bruised ego, m'lady?" he teased. If he was surprised to find her inexperienced in the gentle arts and, in all probability, that he was the first man to have thoroughly kissed her, he never let on.

"How dare you!"

"Indeed!" he scoffed back. "I know better than to think that you are a shrinking violet, so save your theatricals. We have used each other, for which I doubt my apology to you would matter. Besides, I'd make a very demanding husband," he laughed mockingly, waiting for her to stop quivering.

"Get out of here," demanded Sundra. "I'll find a way to the vicarage myself!"

"And leave without collecting the kiss you said that I would always remember? No, m'lady, I stand firm and hold you to your promise."

Sundra was aghast, realizing she stood a better chance escaping from a highwayman than his lordship, unless she were to concede in order for him to leave her in peace.

Sundra never knew what possessed her arms to impulsively reach out and touch Gardner's chest. As he stepped closer, she put her arms around his neck and waited for his lips to reach hers first.

She closed her eyes so tightly, it hurt. His lips were brushing against her cheek. She shivered, not having the slightest idea of what to do next. When she drew in a deep breath and held it, she heard him chuckle softly in her ear.

"Relax against me," he coaxed her. "I'll not harm you."

Sundra had no say in the matter, for while she was contemplating the thought, her body impulsively obliged him.

Gardner tenderly caressed her lips, evoking a passionate response she never knew existed.

The flutter in her stomach, the subtle kneading sensations within her body, left her trembling in awe. She had a taste of love's rare pleasure and, after Gardner disappeared from her life, she knew, regretfully, that it would never happen to her again.

"Perhaps I am a fool . . ." the duke admitted under his breath. He held Sundra an arm's length away, letting the fresh wind clear his head. "Now then, my little dreamer," he remarked. "Be quick to prepare for the journey, and remember to keep your pretty head out of the clouds so you can see where you are going." His gibe bordered on a reproach. "Honestly, you act as though you're blind, or some other such nonsense!"

"What!" Sundra cried too late, for the duke had abruptly deserted her and Addie was now standing bewildered in his place. She had to pry the girl loose from the spot. Quickly, and without a word between them, she guided Sundra back to the manor.

Addie wondered if she had made a mistake by keeping the negligee Alice had thrown at her, spending weeks altering the fashion just to give it to Sundra as a parting gift. Addie watched Sundra holding onto the box, unaware of its contents, while her hands trembled. Instead of being delighted, Sundra appeared to be fuming.

Addie shook her head at Sundra's strange behavior. She was certain the girl hadn't the slightest notion she had wed the dashing stranger from London, who had captured her young girl's imagination. Sundra was better off without him because her face had portrayed a powerful emotion; building castles in the air after she had tangled with the duke. Even if Sundra were to admit her true sentiments, Addie was certain it would lead to no good. She was suspicious that if the duke were serious about love, he would have married long ago!

"He doesn't know I'm blind," Sundra suddenly cried out. "No wonder he thought I acted like a fool! He probably thinks I was making eyes at him when I stared," she sobbed in aggravation. "He had the nerve to suggest that I wanted the dowry for myself! I still have my pride, you know. Oh, Addie, I have a horrible feeling he wasn't given a proper explanation."

"Hush now, child," calmed Addie. "Considering how frantic all of us were yesterday, I think Sir Edmund's explanation was somehow lost upon the wind."

"I must settle the matter and tell His Grace that I'm blind . . . for my own sake, as well as his."

"I don't see what difference it could make now, but if it'll make you feel better, then go ahead and explain."

Addie heard the horses whinnying in the courtyard below.

She tucked her shawl and carpetbag underneath her arm and hobbled over to Sundra.

"'Tis time for me to go," said Addie, her voice strained with emotion.

"I'll miss you very much, Addie dear. Oh, I wish you could come with me! I wish . . ."

"Lud, child! Those grand wishes of yours," teased the maid, trying to ease the agony of parting with the girl she couldn't have loved better even if she were her own daughter. "You better take good care of yourself, missy, because I expect you to get back your eyesight by the time I come to visit!"

Sundra and Addie hugged each other, each straining to giggle farewell lest their tears should fall. The girl dearly thanked the maid for the present and promised to open it after she was safely settled in the vicarage.

"One day you'll have good use for it. Mind that you don't leave it behind when His Grace comes to fetch you," chortled Addie, hurrying from the room.

While Sundra was trying to think of a way to break the news of her blindness to the duke, she heard his footsteps coming up the rear corridor.

Automatically she touched her wedding ring, feeling the odd shape for the first time since it had been placed on her third finger. She made a mental note to have Sir Edmund return it to his lordship after the annulment was made final.

Sundra didn't have the courage to turn and face Gardner when she heard him enter her chamber.

"I wasn't expecting you to come so soon," she said, controlling her quivering voice. "Your Grace, I have something important to tell you . . ."

"So, 'tis Your Grace now, is it? Ha hah," he laughed wickedly, his voice rising from a husky tone to a high pitch as he ogled the gentle curves of her breast that the delicate portions of lace failed to cover. "You're a sly little vixen after all!"

"Elliot!"

"You were expecting the King, perchance?" Elliot had the

nerve to gall. "Come now, what is it you wish to tell me? Hmmm," he droned. Seeing that Sundra had dressed far in advance for their wedding, he reached his own conclusions. "Do you wish to ask for my manly favors so soon?" he laughed jauntily. "Your eagerness pleases me, it does!"

Elliot flew across the room before Sundra had a chance to hear him coming and dodge out of his way. His arms locked around her, making her body a prisoner within his crushing embrace. As his ruddy tongue flicked inside and out of his mouth, wetting his lips, he vowed to extract dozens of kisses from her rosy lips in record-breaking time.

Elliot had been deprived of Miriam's lovemaking far too long. Tonight, when she had refused him again, was the last straw. Since Miriam was up to her ears in champagne and, no doubt, had fallen asleep at his townhouse, he followed his hunch by coming to Bradtree after easy prey.

The strong odor of brandy on Elliot's breath made Sundra panic. She pounded on his chest with her fists, twisting wildly against him to escape his drunken clutches.

"Be still, you little minx," he moaned, his stomach bulging and rumbling against her waist.

"Please, Elliot! You don't know what you're doing!"

"Oh, but I do, I do," he puffed. "Don't tease me! You're dressed for our wedding, and just as anxious to steal a few kisses as I am, only you're too shy to admit it."

"Leave me alone! Stop!" she cried out, her temper flaring. "I know all about your scheme and how you were going to get my money and do away with me! I have just come from the chapel, and I am now legally married to the Duke of Trentbay."

"Arghh," he spat, roughly shoving her away. "Why you little twit! I'll teach you a lesson for ruining my future!"

Elliot retrieved his walking stick and charged after Sundra. His first attempt at swinging the cane merely grazed her shoulder. She fell backward across a footstool.

Sundra was yanked to her feet. The harder she struggled, the more excited he became. A blow to her shins caused tears of pain to slide down her cheeks. She was terrified of what was yet to come because she couldn't see to thwart his attack.

She felt the perspiration from his palm being kneaded into her skin as his fingers dug into her arm while he was trying to hold her still. He flogged her backside several times.

When Elliot suddenly stopped, Sundra thought he was taking a breather before continuing his thrashing. She prayed for mercy.

It was then, during her brief interlude of faith, that she heard the nearby click of a primed pistol.

"Release her!" Gardner's demand was cold and ominous. "I've no wish to see your blood touching the lady when I kill you."

In between his coughs of blasphemy, Sundra heard the baronet rustling toward the mantel, gasping for air.

"Damn you, Foxworthy! How dare you barge in here," bellowed Elliot as he tore off his cravat. "You've no right to intrude. Where the hell did you come from, anyway!"

"Speak your piece, Spencer, for I will not tolerate your degrading actions against Lady Sundra."

"Lud! The chit's unharmed, with no thanks to you," raged Elliot, losing control of his boyish temper. "If Lady Miriam sent you here as some sort of a joke, it can end right now!"

Elliot thought it was just like Miriam to spite him at the eleventh hour. She probably knew about his intentions all along and had sent Foxworthy here as her watchdog to spoil his innocent fun, mocking his masculinity.

Although Gardner had instantly earned a special place in her heart for saving her, Sundra's blood ran cold when she had heard that the duke intended to kill Elliot on her account.

"Don't fight," she cried. "Please Gardner, you mustn't jeopardize your future because of me. I'll be fine, if only you'll send him away."

"Be silent, woman," warned Elliot as he cleared his throat. "I don't want this matter to get out of hand. I'm willing to let bygones be bygones," he said diplomatically. "'Tis obvious

Sundra has told us a pack of lies, although I don't think it's any of your business. Just leave the chit to me and I'll straighten her out but good."

"Had I the time, I would cut out your heart," Gardner claimed, a dangerous glint in his eyes. "Sundra belongs to me and I have every intention of keeping her to myself. She is my wife!"

The duke spoke with such malice and authority that Elliot was struck dumb by the cold truth; an irrefutable truth, for a Foxworthy was as good as his word.

The baronet blanched, his heart banging with trepidation. He watched in spellbound silence as the duke raised his arm and accurately aimed the pistol at his heart. Slowly his legs buckled and caused his rotund body to melt into a truckle position upon the floor.

At this point Sundra sensed that her plea for mercy could not prevent the duke from avenging her attack. Acting on a sudden impulse she lunged precariously in Gardner's direction, hoping as her body fell against his she might prevent a further act of violence from taking place.

Sundra's move had been too sudden. Lightheaded and blindly disoriented, she careened off the side of Gardner's arm and staggered into the line of fire just as the pistol exploded. The bullet grazed the side of her head but completely missed hitting Elliot.

Gardner swooped Sundra into his arms as she crumpled in front of him; her body was totally limp. He watched Elliot go streaking from the room, acting every bit the cur he was. The duke didn't give a damn. His only concern was for Sundra, who had risked her life to save him from his own anger.

Gardner was relieved Sundra's wound was superficial, although his heart had skipped a beat when she first went down, and before he knew she had merely fainted.

He frowned when he noticed the other lump on her temple, wondering what kind of trouble had she gotten into to have caused her injury.

Sundra's first thought upon awakening was to escape from Elliot, unaware Gardner was holding her tight.

"Easy, my little one," calmed Gardner. "You shouldn't move until I can take a good look at your wound."

"Oh, sir," she whimpered. "Are you all right? H-has Elliot . . ."

"Shh! He's gone from your life forever. Now, if you'll lie still, I'll hurry and fetch Addie."

"No . . . don't leave me, Your Grace . . . please . . . hold me . . ."

The duke looked into her tear-filled eyes, which slowly closed against her will. "You foolish little romantic," he whispered to her, gently brushing aside a tumbled lock as he kissed her. "Your fiery spirit, I'm convinced, will be too strong for you to control in the future," mused Gardner, assuming the petite bundle he was holding would, in due time, cause a peck of trouble for her guardian. A challenging thought, indeed!

Gardner heard the patter of running footsteps and turned around just in time to face a breathless young woman.

"And whom might you be," he inquired in a harsh voice.

"I'm Miriam, Lady Bradford, Sundra's cousin and stepmother," she cried. "Has Elliot done this to her?"

"You sound as though you expected as much!"

Mariam covered her face in shame. "This is all my fault! I arranged to have Sundra wed Elliot tomorrow. I sensed he was getting out of hand, but why would he do such a cruel thing on the eve of his wedding?"

"Perhaps he was livid when he found out that Sundra and I are man and wife," answered the duke coldly, glancing menacingly at the intruder. "'Tis St. Ives's day, is it not! Now if you'll excuse me, I must deliver Sundra to the vicarage before my ship sails in the morning for Canada."

The realization Miriam would be left alone and penniless in the world brought her to her knees. She'd be headed for Tyburn Prison before the day was out!

"Please wait," she begged, throwing herself in front of the duke to block his path. "I know who you are, Your Grace. How Sundra arranged this match, I'll never know, but I beg of you not to leave her and me behind! Elliot will seek revenge on both of us," she claimed cleverly, knowing she must use Sundra as bait in order to look after her own well-being. "I know you are a man of honor who would not willingly leave us helpless women to the mercy of a deranged fortune hunter or the street-runners. Take us with you . . . I beg of you!"

CHAPTER 5

Gardner was braced on the *Northwind*'s quarterdeck, supervising the ship's passage into the channel. With any luck they would be able to drop anchor a half mile south of Spithead shortly after dawn.

"Beggin' yer pardon, Capt'n."

"What is it now, Briggs," shouted Gardner, his voice sounding loud and clear against the flapping spanker. This was the fourth time the old bosun had come up to pester him, as if the groaning creaks in the rigging weren't enough to make him short-tempered; not to mention sailing through the dead of night with nary a star to guide him.

"Sir Jamie gave the men yer orders," Briggs managed to say without choking on a mouthful of tobacco. "Mistress Coralee's got yer lady settled in real cozy like. Heard she was restin' a mite better, but she's still conked out. Guess I'd be too," he sniffed, "if I was knocked on the noggin like she was!"

Briggs saw the captain glaring down at him. He stopped chewing on his wad, nearly swallowing it, and gave him a bewildered shrug.

"Very well," sighed Gardner. "Stand ready to help Miss Tubbins in case she needs anything else from the ship's store. Report back to me the minute there's been a change in my wife's condition."

"Aye, Capt'n, that I'll do!"

Instead of going below, Briggs leaned on the railing and started picking his fingernails with a penknife he had used earlier to slice a wedge of cheese.

"Ye know, Capt'n, all the years I've been with ye and Jamie Moore, we've called each other every blasted name under the sun," Briggs said with a snort. "But fer the life o' me, I don't know what's proper fer me to call yer wife, 'cause ye ain't never been married/afore," he added seriously.

Gardner had been in a dark mood ever since he had left Bradtree, and this moment wasn't any different. He didn't want to discuss his personal life or have Briggs prodding him about Sundra, troubled because he had married without concern for his family honor or the consequences of a convenient annulment.

He had risked Sundra's life and reputation in order to gain her dowry. With no thanks to him, he had placed her in further jeopardy by bringing her on board instead of taking her to the vicarage, to throw Elliot off her trail just in case.

The less said about husband and wife being innocently together the better, he thought. Nothing was going to hamper the annulment proceedings and he was going to make sure Sundra was quickly deposited on the Wellses' doorstep before anyone, Lady Miriam included, formulated an idea to delay their permanent separation.

The duke returned his attention to scowl at Briggs. "I don't have time to answer your asinine question! Now get your rump over to the galley and tell Mr. Potts to prepare grog for the men. I don't like the feel of this wind."

The captain's quarters kept out threatening weather throughout the night while Sundra was slowly recovering from her traumatic stupor.

Knowing she had received far more than her share of bumps and bruises, she did not think it odd that she was swaying dizzily in bed, or that a rolling ship had anything to do with her askew position.

Sundra's head and eyes were swathed in a soft cloth dampened with scented water. She lifted her arm, reaching up to her cheek to push back a bothersome fold.

Swiftly another hand gently moved the bandage for her.

"Don't be scared, Sunny. 'Tis Coralee, and I've been taking real good care of you."

"Coralee!" Sundra sounded relieved. "Ooh . . . my head . . . hurts." She paused for a moment, listening, and urging her senses to take stock of the situation.

"Lean back on your pillow," Coralee cautioned her. "You've been out cold for quite a spell and I don't want you passin' out again." Coralee sat on the edge of the bed and tucked the quilt over Sundra's shoulders. "Bet that makes you feel better."

"Yes, feels nice and warm," Sundra murmured, and then gasped, "Aunt Grace! S-she must be frantic to have seen me like this. Oh, Coralee, was she terribly upset when she called for your help?"

"Mrs. Wells doesn't know about this. I mean, we're not at the vicarage."

"But . . . I d-don't understand!"

"We're on board His Grace's ship and we're sailing down the middle of the English Channel," explained Coralee. Who'd have believed she would ever run into Sundra again!

Coralee had lived on the farm adjoining the foundling home and had been Sundra's companion since they were ten years old. Recently, when Sundra had hastily ended her three-month visit and left the vicarage, they had no chance to say farewell. According to rumors, Coralee never expected to ever see her again.

"Sir James told me His Grace brought you along until he thinks it's safe for you to join the Wellses."

"I appreciate his concern, but where is he taking me? And why are you on this ship? How did you . . ."

"You're not to worry yourself, 'cause I'll be the one who gits a sound scolding if you do! His lordship is attending to urgent business down by Spithead." Coralee went on to say that after Sundra was taken back to the country, the ship was sailing to Canada, where she was going to start a new life for herself. "You see, Sunny, my father was killed when his wagon overturned during the storm, the same day I heard that you left the vicarage," Coralee said sadly. "I ran away from Uncle Tim's."

Timothy Tubbins had quickly disposed of Coralee's farm and

had taken her in. He had different ideas about how she was going to earn her keep, and it wasn't merely waiting on tables at the Black Douglas Inn that he had in mind.

Coralee had remembered Sir James's standing offer to be of assistance if she ever needed it, and went to him for help. Willingly she indentured her services to the Duke of Trentbay in return for her passage out of the country.

"I'm truly very sorry, Coralee."

"No more than I am to have heard on the servants' grapevine about the troubles you're going through. Poor Lord Giles," Coralee cried, covering her sobs with her starched apron.

Sundra didn't have the heart to add to Coralee's misery by admitting she was going to spend the rest of her life in a darkened world. Coralee would take pity on her, and then doubts and insecurity would creep over her once again.

Coralee sensed a change in Sundra. She had to alter the conversation before it put a damper on Sundra's spirits. She reached for the shears and announced it was time to remove the bandage, smiling when Sundra gave a sigh of relief to be freed of the sopping herb cloth.

"Keep your eyes shut tight until I wipe away the salve," she coaxed, commenting how well the wound appeared after the first treatment.

When Sundra finally opened her eyes, she nearly lost her breath! "Oh, Coralee!" she cried loudly. "I can see again!"

If Coralee was puzzled by her comment, she was thoroughly perplexed when Sundra threw away the covers and stared at the cabin in amazement, acting as though she had never seen one before in her life!

The men pushed aside their chairs in the day cabin as they prepared to go up on deck.

"You're not coming with me and that's final," announced Gardner irately. "If I fail to show up after an hour, don't waste your time looking for me. Just take Sundra back to the vicarage where she belongs."

James punched the palm of his hand with his clenched fist.

Where Sundra belongs, indeed! If Gardner had taken her to the rectory in the first place, he'd be able to go ashore with the duke. Damned if he knew how their plans got so muddled with ifs and buts! "Ah, the devil take me," fumed James. Like it or not, he was saddled with the responsibility of commanding the ship during Gardner's absence.

"What the hell did you expect me to do with Sundra after she was attacked?" Gardner replied in a deep voice. "I couldn't afford to waste my time to explain to the Reverend Wells why my wife, whom I was deserting, was in such a sorry state."

A rogue he might be, but a heartless fool? Never! For what little time Sundra had with him, intending to leave Sundra and Miriam to start anew in England while he returned home to his Canadian estate, he was adamant about providing her with his protection. He owed her that much, if nothing else.

James was having second thoughts about Gardner's marriage and the insensitive way the young girl was being treated. 'Tis a convenience for Gardner but surely not for Sundra, he thought regretfully.

The helmsman's gruff voice reverberated along the companionway. The *Northwind* had reached her destination. Gardner and James went topside, facing the red sky in the morning with indifference.

The wind had puffed out to sea, leaving the channel calm enough to reflect the sun's image as a steadfast ruby against the quelled surface. A shroud of nipping air from the northwest had settled in. Beneath the wispy patches of the rising mist the change in the water temperature went undetected.

Windy and Clyde had no problem holding the rowboat steady against the hull as Gardner climbed down the rope ladder and jumped in. Silent and steady, determination wrinkling their brows, they set their chapped hands in the oars with practiced ease and shoved off without delay.

James ordered the crew to stand ready at their stations. Tobey signaled to him from the crow's nest that he had a clear view of the captain's destination and would observe the meeting with his spyglass. If Gardner were in trouble, a drop of his skullcap would send the rugged backup crew into immediate action.

"Briggs." James beckoned, his boots planted firmly apart as he stood vigil. "Post yourself outside the lady's cabin. No one is permitted to enter, or leave. Do I make myself clear?"

The bosun eyed James suspiciously, knowing full well the first mate issued those orders because he didn't trust Deacon lurking below deck.

Dirty Deacon, as his shipmates had dubbed him by pouring a mug of ale over his stinking head to welcome him aboard, had recently signed on to replace the ship's carpenter. He was a bit grubby, wearing dirt-starched clothes, but he had made friends with the bosun and other crewmen stationed below.

"Jamie wants an old foozle like me out of the way," he muttered out loud. "The young buck doesn't think I knows what he's hankerin' fer?" he asked himself with a chuckle, knowing that Sir James would find a way to bend the captain's orders to go ashore if the duke happened to get waylaid. "Ho ho, what a scrapper! Find a fight an' ye'll find Jamie Moore!" A smile spread across his leathered face. Just like the good old days, he thought.

Briggs trudged below and managed to check on the women. All went well except when he had to stop Mistress Tubbins from going to the galley. He thought she looked cute, getting all ruffled up when he wouldn't let her pass. He must not have heard being asked to leave, because the chit slammed the door in his face, nearly smacking the wood against his bulbous nose.

"Oh, Coralee! When I asked you to shut the door, I didn't mean for you to knock that poor old man off his feet."

"Serves him right!" replied Coralee. "Wants us to come to no harm, yet he was holding the door wide open for any bugger to ramble in here! I wonder if the other woman passenger was treated in the same unchivalrous way."

Coralee had overheard that the duke had left the ship and was upset because she missed the chance to inform him about the change in Sundra's condition. Now they were locked inside without a drop of tea or a crust of bread, she was angered that Sunny must go without nourishment until his lordship returned.

"Come sit next to me, Coralee. His Grace will return soon and then you'll be able to tell him."

"Aye, I guess I'm too excited about giving him such splendid news."

"Please promise you won't say a word about my blindness. I'd rather he hear it from me, so I can be sure of explaining why I acted so foolhardy at Bradtree."

The only thought comforting Sundra was that Coralee knew nothing about the wicked plans Miriam and Elliot had had in store for her. It was a painful part of her past which she never wanted to recall again.

"A marriage of convenience must be hard for you to accept. When I think of all those rainy afternoons we hid in the hayloft and dreamed about the future, well, I know how much you wanted to marry for love or not at all."

"For once in my life I'm going to pay attention to what money can do for me," Sundra said, in order to center the conversation on her new goal in life. "There'll be no stopping me now since I've regained my eyesight."

Sundra was going to London in style to associate with Quality who could afford to champion the cause of needy orphans. She was going to place the older children with decent tradesmen. For the toddlers she would purchase warm clothing and perhaps a toy. Above all else, she would make certain all of them received the one thing money could never buy—love.

"Bless you, Sunny. I'm going to miss seeing your wishes come true," Coralee cried softly. "You've a kind heart and I'll pray the church'll understand about your forthcoming annulment."

Sundra knew the duke was making her mission possible. He would never realize the depth of her gratitude. For his sake, she wasn't going to delay signing the annulment. Let him be free as he'd always wanted to be.

"Let's celebrate," chortled Coralee. "When the door's unlocked, I'll fetch a pot of tea," she laughed and added on a cheerful note, "and we'll make a toast to our new future, and to His Grace, for making it all possible! 'Ere, would you like me to go with you when you talk with his lordship?"

"No," replied Sundra shyly. "I think I can trust him for the few minutes it takes me to settle matters between us."

"Just as I thought," giggled Coralee. "You may have married the Duke of Trentbay, but how are you going to find him? La, silly Sunny, you've never even 'seen' your husband!"

Sundra laughed at Coralee's humor, but deep down inside she felt like crying—and didn't know why.

Gardner was on his way back to the ship within the alotted time. The oarsmen had their backs to the wind, which was darting across the channel with renewed vigor, stirring the water into shallow parallels of choppy waves. James could see the wicked scowl on Gardner's face. Something had gone awry at Spithead.

The crew scurried on deck with accomplished speed to receive their captain. Gardner flung aside his canvas slicker and went charging across the deck.

"Have Briggs pick out nine men to secure the cargo. Order the rest to their quarters. I want a fresh crew ready tonight when I give the command," ordered Gardner, holding a crumpled piece of paper as he cursed his way past James.

Worried, James swiftly ran after the duke, thinking they shouldn't plan to sail off again in the night, not with a storm brewing! "What's happened?" he asked uneasily.

"The turnkey raised his price! I'm to return with the full payment at three o'clock in the morning. I'll explain it all to you in the day cabin," he growled.

After Briggs had been called for other duties, Coralee was free to go to the galley. She grabbed up the bottom hem of her apron and dashed down the passageway, hoping she might be able to talk Mr. Potts out of a special treat he might have hidden away.

She was bright-eyed and rosy cheeked as she sped around the corner, eager to be on her merry way. Her gallop was most unladylike, and she'd never have dared to expose her ankles had she known the duke was watching her as he descended the staircase.

Alarmed, Gardner forgot about the remaining steps and lunged toward Coralee as she scampered within reach, catching hold of her arm with a steel grip.

"Sundra!" Gardner bellowed his first thought without realizing he had raised his voice. "Has she . . ."

"She's fine," squeaked Coralee. "Believe me, I was about to tell you the good news before you left, but I couldn't get to you in time, Your Grace!"

Gardner let go of her arm and turned away. "You were told not to leave her side!" His voice was threatening.

"I didn't mean to, sir, but I wanted to fetch some tea for our celebration." Coralee shifted her weight from one foot to the other, unnerved when the duke turned and reproached her with a cold stare.

"Has it not occurred to you, Miss Tubbins," he exclaimed, "that your patient might not be as fit as you'd like to think she is? After what Sundra's been through, I doubt if she has enough strength to hold a teacup, celebration or not," Gardner said arrogantly.

"But, sir, she's made a remarkable recovery, I tell you!" Coralee replied quickly. "You wouldn't worry if you'd have seen how happy she's been this past hour, bubbling about returning to London in style and all! Especially since she's regained . . ."

"Regained what?" demanded Gardner.

"I'm sorry, Your Grace." Coralee lowered her eyes, twisting her apron string into a knot. "I promised her I wouldn't tell a soul. She says she'll personally explain everything to you, later on."

"I see," commented the duke, his face turning a shade darker. "James, see that a pot of tea is delivered to my wife's cabin for her celebration," he said curtly, dismissing him with a cynical smile. "Now, Miss Tubbins," he drawled, offering his arm. "Will you permit me a few moments of your time?"

Astounded, Coralee accepted with pleasure and was led into the day cabin by the strongest arm she had ever touched. She was proud his lordship was treating her with cordial respect, and was willing to show her obedience and gratitude to her new employer as best she could.

The duke gestured for her to sit directly in front of him. "I understand you've been friends with Sundra since you were children," he began, giving Coralee the opportunity to relax while he poured brandy into his snifter. "I suppose she's told you about her . . . illness?"

Coralee was inwardly pleased with the duke for taking enough interest by asking for her opinions. He was such an honorable man!

"You are jesting with me, Your Grace." She respectfully admonished him with a giggle. "Sunny's never been sick in all the days I've known her," she replied coyly.

"A toast to her health then," conceded Gardner, draining the liquor from his glass. "Surely, Miss Tubbins, we can stop pretending and admit we know the truth about her secret ailment which plagued her recently." The duke narrowed his eyes to judge her reaction.

"Oh, that!" Coralee blushed profusely, embarrassed she hadn't realized by now that nothing escaped the duke's attention. "You only know half the story, Your Grace, and I beg that you not think poorly of me for breaking my promise to Sunny."

"You are doing nothing more than what is expected of you, Miss Tubbins. Honesty is a requirement, if you wish to remain on my staff," Gardner commented sternly, and settled into an overstuffed chair, his eyes piercing the side of his glass while he drank. The outcome of his fermenting rage was resting on the balance of the girl's story.

"We both know what a sorry state Sunny was in when you brought her on board. A change came over her the minute I took the bandage away from her eyes. She was so happy to see those beautiful paintings that she tiptoed and touched every color!" The memory filled Coralee with emotion. "The way she handled the leather books, a golden inkwell, velvet chairs, and the handsome trappings in the salon, brought a lump to my throat. I cried when she told me she had recovered. She said it was a complicated story and wished to break the news to you herself."

"So, her 'miraculous' recovery is why you want to celebrate," Gardner asked astutely.

"Only part," admitted Coralee. "Sunny's going to make a toast to the future, and to you, for making her wish come true."

The brandy did not sit well in Gardner's stomach.

Coralee was alarmed to see the duke's eyes blazing in obvious anger, feeling a chill rush over her. "Y-your G-grace!" She stumbled over the words. "Please, I'm begging you not to be harsh with Sunny for not telling you everything before you left Bradtree. 'Course, by then, you were already wed and I doubt that her story would have changed matters," she sighed. "Sunny is a sensitive girl, her pride's been injured. I think she's desperately counting on you to understand her predicament. Oh, forgive me, Your Grace! Have I spoken out of line?" Coralee trembled out of control, sensing the room was in a lull before the storm.

"Stop making that chair rattle," Gardner demanded sharply. "I'm not going to beat you!"

Was Miss Tubbins such a complete idiot as to admit he had been duped into marriage by a girl who feigned an illness, cleverly employing Sir Edmund to snare him legally, or somehow using Lady Miriam's plighty story to aid her scheme?

Sundra already had his titled name, Gardner regretted. No telling what sort of deviltry she'd be up to if she could manage to use it to her advantage.

He was a fool to think she believed the marriage vows were sacred. Who was she to care if the annulment dissolved their union—there was nothing in their contract that forbade her from keeping his name. How convenient! A titled name, a sizable dowry share; to bandy them on the streets of London without a husband to stop her, making him a laughingstock of the courts!

Gardner drained the last mouthful of brandy and abruptly flung the empty glass against the wall, unable to restrain the anger inside him.

"I'll be damned if I do, and damned if I don't," he raged.

Startled, Coralee fell off her seat, then scrambled midway to the door. Her eyes were big as saucers. She hid two shaking hands beneath her starched apron.

"Consider yourself freed of the indentured bond, Miss Tubbins," Gardner said as a matter of fact. "From now on, you will serve as my wife's personal maid, and you'll receive a wage befitting the station you now hold in my service."

"Please have mercy on me, Your Grace," sobbed Coralee. "I'm deathly afraid of what'll happen if I step foot in London."

"What, may I ask, ever gave you the idea you'll be returning to that city?" he asked arrogantly.

"I must go wherever my mistress leads me, and Sunny intends to go there straightaway!"

"Indeed!" Gardner scoffed harshly, swiftly rising from his chair. "Sundra is my wife, and I don't intend to let her out of my sight, much less grant her an annulment," he snarled, walking on the broken glass, deliberately crushing the pieces into the planked floor as he stalked over to the sideboard.

"Your Grace is taking her to Canada?" she asked, her voice quivering with astonishment.

"Whether she likes it or not," snapped Gardner.

The menacing look on the duke's face made Coralee edge closer toward the door. Flustered, she nodded in agreement and curtsied before him, a blush speckling her worried face.

"Briggs will move your belongings elsewhere, and you may inform my little 'defender-of-the-scared-vows' wife to get used to the idea of sharing a cabin with her husband." The duke flashed her an all-knowing smile. "Leave!"

With tears in her eyes, Coralee bolted out of the cabin, convinced that somehow Sunny had just lost her precious freedom.

"Really, Gardner!" Sir James bantered as he came striding into the room. "Frightening off the women again, are you?"

"On the contrary, James. I've decided against the annulment. I'm taking Sundra back with me to Tamarack," Gardner stated flatly, preparing a missive to Dilly and the Wellses.

"You don't say! And what brought about this sudden change of heart," prodded James, "a guilty conscience?" Thoroughly delighted, he slapped the side of his leg and laughed. "Lud! If that's all it took, I can imagine what Alice will have to say about your honorable intentions. When I think of all the times that woman harped my ear off, hoping I could persuade you to become a respectable married man! Why, you hellion!" he guffawed. "You've the luck of the devil to have wed such an innocent flower, and well you know it!"

"Damn you," Gardner replied acidly, "enough said about my wife! I'm not ridding myself of her, but I didn't say I liked the idea. And my sister's matchmaking whims had nothing to do with my decision either!"

A storm was approaching and the ship was beginning to pitch in the rapidly rising waves. The crumpled paper the duke had carried back from Spithead slid across the tabletop.

As quickly as he had snatched up the paper and read it, James threw it down on the floor, his face contorted into a disgusted frown. "The price is doubled! This means you'll be forced to use all of Sundra's dowry, damn it," he fumed. "Are you vexed because she agreed to live with you because she couldn't afford to go back to London? . . . No!" he corrected himself. "I don't believe a lady as kind as she could be so callous."

The duke merely ignored James's last remark, casting his menacing eyes in his direction.

"It is not my wish to involve Sundra in my personal affairs," Gardner deliberately drawled in a bored tone. "She doesn't know I've seized her fortune or for what purpose I intend to use it, nor should she be concerned even if she did know. Sundra is my wife," he continued mockingly, "and I expect her to obey the decisions I've made for her."

"Lud, Gardner!" James eyed him suspiciously. "Are you forcing Sundra to stay married to you against her wishes?"

After his instructions had been penned, and the contents of

the pouch of gold were spread and ready to be counted, Gardner looked up and faced his contentious friend.

"I should think attending elegant parties or a tavern brawl would be enough to keep you busy," sneered Gardner. "Until those men are freed, I'll not discuss my wife or my motives with someone who should know better than to stick his nose where it doesn't belong!"

With torrents of rain pelting heavily against the ship, Gardner and James raised their voices, locked in another of their heated debates.

"The devil take it," roared James. "Your behavior of late has much to be desired! You're so concerned to give those prisoners their freedom that your cocksure attitude is taking its toll of your better judgment. I'm damned right to side against you."

"To hell with you then! Those men remain loyal to my family. I cannot stand idle while their hands are lopped off for stealing moldy bread from the gutter, a crime which they didn't commit. If you're as eager to see justice served, then come with me. And heaven help you if Briggs sails the *Northwind* aground while we're ashore!"

" 'Tis not the point," argued James, realizing he was as much at fault as the duke. "We should have demanded proof that the men will be on the beach. Now you're forced to hand over all of Sundra's dowry, and what will you get? Some bastard's word of honor about where those poor buggers are hiding? You may be in danger. Are they that important to smuggle back home to work on Alice's homestead? Lud," he scoffed, "believe me, if all this fuss was for 'Alice Rose,' I wouldn't lift a finger!"

James angrily started to shove fistfuls of guineas into the pouch, eager to head for shore, but the duke was not paying any attention to him. Gardner was watching the door!

They heard a scuffle in the hallway. Someone was listening!

The wooden hull moaned as a giant wave crashed against it, causing the ship to list precariously to the starboard side.

The person standing outside the day cabin was thrown against the door. It opened and, with a flurry of swirling lace and flounces, Sundra tumbled inside.

Without saying a word, James, who was nearer, helped her to her feet.

Keeping her eyes cast down to the floor, Sundra slapped the folds of her skirt into place, paying more attention to her semblance than was necessary.

As she stood in full view she had the dreadful feeling that the men, one being her husband, must think she had been eavesdropping on their private conversation.

It wasn't her fault she heard a few loud remarks while she stood trembling outside, mustering her courage to knock.

"Thank you," she said, looking gratefully at James. Remembering it wasn't polite to keep one's back turned, Sundra stepped aside to glance at the other gentleman. Her body suddenly straighted and grew stiff when she recognized him.

"You!" Sundra exclaimed indignantly, making sense of the overheard conversation. That man, she remembered angrily, had been a thorn in her side ever since she had encountered him escorting that odious Alice!

Sundra's eyes wandered back to James, whom she immediately mistook as her husband. He had argued with the arrogant stranger about giving away her dowry. The mere mention of the paramour's name, Alice, was making her temper flair all the more.

She wanted the annulment, her share of the dowry and most of all, she wanted to get away from the stranger whose eyes were roving over her body this very moment!

"Your Grace, please order that gentleman to leave," she demanded, drawing closer to James while pointing her finger at the man she wanted dismissed. "There are important matters which we must have settled between us, in private."

"Cat got your tongue, Jamie?" remarked Gardner, a hardened smile playing across his face. He tilted back in his chair until he was braced against the paneled wall. "My wife," he commented coldly, watching the color drain from Sundra's face, "has asked you to leave us alone."

When Sundra heard the London stranger speak, she knew the voice belonged to the man she had married! He once held her, kissed her, and she had felt a strange desire growing within after experiencing his embrace. The fact sent shivers running down her spine. If ever there was a time she could make herself faint into oblivion, it was now. Why, oh why, hadn't Addie warned her!

"May I please sit down?" she begged in a whisper, watching an embarrassed James bowing nervously as he took his leave.

Gardner leaned forward and booted a chair toward her as though he was annoyed to have made the effort.

"Perhaps you can explain why you addressed James Moore as your husband. Wishful thinking? Or are you addlebrained from your so-called illness," taunted Gardner.

"I came here to explain, to come to terms," she snapped. "I'll not be dragged through the mud, and certainly not by you!"

Gardner folded his arms across his chest and yawned, clearly uninterested in what she had to say.

Sundra knew if she didn't start explaining she would lose the only chance she had for freedom. She mustn't get into a shouting match with the likes of him!

"Your Grace," began Sundra, controlling the tone of her voice. "I was blind at the time of our marriage," she confessed, "and my eyesight has only returned a short while ago. It was my mistake to think Sir James was my husband. I mean, I never thought I could ever have married someone like . . . you." Her last word was barely a whisper, but audible to the duke's keen sense of hearing.

"Sir Edmund promised you would know about my plight before the contract was signed. But after the ceremony, I realized that you didn't know. My pride is the only reason why I'm telling you now. I didn't want you to think I was a stumbling schoolgirl."

"How you acted at the chapel doesn't concern me in the least. I thought I made it quite clear to Miss Tubbins that you've played the last of your charades. So, you've got the light back in your eyes, supposedly," he mocked, "and you have me! Remember? The vows are sacred? Don't tell me that you've changed your mind about the church laws now that I'm not going to abuse them!"

If the contempt in his voice wasn't enough to frighten Sundra, the look of rage on his darkened face certainly was. She started to cry, but only because he had heard her arguing with Addie at the chapel and had drawn the wrong conclusion from it.

The duke was maliciously accusing her of trapping him and she was fighting a losing battle trying to convince him otherwise. It was her word against his.

Sundra's sweet tears of misery turned bitter by the time the droplets touched her trembling lips.

"I don't care what you think of me," she said sarcastically, trying to avoid looking into his eyes. "I want the annulment and my rightful share of the dowry."

The duke merely snickered at her demands. "Depending on my mood, I may allow you to shop in Quebec or Montreal. Wish as you may, there won't be many occasions to use such frippery in the wilderness, as you'll soon find out."

"Oh!" she cried in horror. Is that what he thought she'd use the money on? Fancy gowns and evening silks she'd never wanted? Of all the nerve!

"If you must know," she said, gritting her teeth, "the Bradfords have supported the Wells foundling home for years. Without my share of the dowry they'll cease to exist. Please, Your Grace, now that my father has passed away, let me help the orphans as best as I can. You've really no right to stop me!"

The duke let the chair fall behind him as he grabbed hold of Sundra and wrenched her from her seat. She felt the hardness of his hands squeezing into her tender flesh.

"Do you think I'm an idiot?" he questioned sharply.

Sundra was being shaken like a rag doll, and obeyed the command for attention by raising her chin to face the duke.

"Even the chimney sweeps in London can vouch that the Prince is responsible for the upkeep of the children's home!"

Sundra closed her eyes, violently shaking her head in disbelief. Miriam had lied to her again! Her story was nothing more than a ruse. The home never needed her money—Miriam did!

"I never want to hear you lie to me again," Gardner said viciously. "You are a Foxworthy. If you can't respect me, then at least have the decency to respect the name I've given you. Other than that, you'll receive precious little from me, my duchess," he mocked ruthlessly.

Sundra fought against Gardner's restraint, knowing as she kicked and squirmed to escape she was caught in another's web of lies and was paying dearly for it.

She didn't understand why the duke wanted to keep her in wedlock. She only knew the duke was too powerful a man for her to resist his final decision. No matter what he said, her freedom was lost to a loveless marriage, her good intentions lost to the wind.

Sundra admitted defeat. She turned passive, leaning her head against Gardner's chest simply because she didn't care what she did anymore.

"You have hurt me more than I'll ever admit," she whimpered softly to him. Without showing her fear, she looked up at her husband's face and gently tilted her head to one side.

"I believe James dislikes Alice as much as I do," she conceded, painfully aware her husband's loyalty lay elsewhere. "As much as I'd like to, I can never forget the cruel way your lady friend Alice treated Addie when we bumped into you on the corner by Madame Rene's shop," she said, bitter tears streaming down her cheeks. "Of course a lady should never know or speak about her husband's liaisons, but if Alice is lurking in the background to share my dowry with you, then you may keep my money. Give it all to her because I don't care! I couldn't hate you more than I do already!"

Let Gardner choke on the very words he was trying to spit out, thought Sundra, picking up her long skirt and stamping away from her stunned husband. Angrily she pulled open the door, slamming it with a bang, and immediately fainted in the passageway.

Gardner stalked after her and found her sprawled in a tiny heap upon the hardwood floor.

"You little hellion," he whispered coarsely as he picked her up and held her close against his body. He frowned. Even in a dead faint, her lips were turned downward at the corners; a pout, no less! His pride was tempered with angered arrogance. He'd be damned if he was going to explain to Sundra that she had confused his sister with a past acquaintance, both sharing the first name of Alice.

"A fortune for Alice Rose's favors, indeed!" he scoffed aloud. Let Sundra think what she liked, he thought, wondering if he had heard correctly the faint traces of jealousy in her voice.

Gardner left Sundra in the care of her maid. Briggs was summoned and once again stood sentinel outside her door.

The blustering storm continued to rage long after the sun had set. During the night the *Northwind* was allowed to drift cautiously toward the shore.

Through pouring rain and perilous waves, the captain and his men rowed with all their might toward the glow of a lantern; the signal leading them to a rendezvous on the beach.

The twelve men, weak and exhausted from the trip from Tyburn, had no problem hauling their emaciated frames into the escape boat. They hadn't exactly been God-fearing men in the past, but each one silently thanked his Maker for giving him a new life and country.

Back on board the *Northwind*, Gardner and James studied the charts throughout the early-morning hours. They were barely civil to each other because they had argued about the way Sundra was being doubted and treated.

When the watchman announced that a gray dawn was appearing, Gardner and James took charge of the ship in strained harmony.

With rain spitting in their faces and the tang of salt permeating the air, the muscled crew labored round the giant capstan. The power of the wind against the mainsail pushed the *Northwind* out of the English Channel and into the arms of the stormy Atlantic.

CHAPTER 6

During the voyage Sundra took advantage of the uneventful days by exploring the lower deck with a curious maid in tow. The duke remained aloof and had not engaged her in conversation since they had left the Channel a week ago. Thus, Briggs acted as messenger and had given Sundra a list of the captain's restrictions. She and Coralee kept a safe distance away from the crew and the vicinity of the gunpowder magazine. They were not allowed on the upper deck because the weather was not fit. Their curiosity grew stronger to catch a glimpse of the other woman passenger, a recluse who shunned even the captain's company.

Contrary to what Gardner had told Coralee, he did not move into his wife's quarters, which Sundra was not about to debate. She received her meals in the solitude of her cabin and oftentimes sent back an untouched tray. When Coralee was dismissed for the evening, Sundra would read books from the duke's library until the wee hours of the morning. She tried to forget her husband, and the hungry way his eyes kept following her whenever she was within spying distance below deck.

Sundra timed her visits with Mr. Potts when he wasn't feeding a hungry troop of men. If he couldn't stuff her with beef pasties he would fill her mind with adventuresome tales. He unknowingly helped ease her loneliness by introducing her to Buster, a black and tan terrier, ship's ratter, and loyal companion to anyone who'd scratch behind his always-alert ears.

Sundra was sipping her breakfast tea. The food on her plate had grown cold.

"What's Mr. Potts going to think if you keep refusing the fine fare he's prepared for you," asked Coralee, shaking her head at the thick slice of ham, boiled potatoes dripping with melted butter, a stack of fluffy biscuits glazed with raspberry jam going to waste. "Mercy sakes," she scolded Sundra, "you want His Grace to hear about this?"

Sundra shot a quizzical glance at her maid. Coralee was trying to scare her into a choice: eat or else stand up to her husband, who would undoubtably force the food down her throat. As if he cared, thought Sundra.

When Coralee turned her back, Sundra snatched the slice of ham and hid it inside the fold of her napkin. She might not have an appetite, but she knew who did! She excused herself by telling Coralee she was going out for a short walk.

As Sundra approached the storage room, concealing Buster's cubbyhole, she heard the dog's vicious snorts and a volley of muffled curses. The man called Deacon was shuffling awkwardly out of the room with Buster hanging fast to the seat of his breeches.

Without warning Deacon took one of the heavier boards he was carrying and used it as a club to beat off the animal before Sundra could stop him. The little dog yelped and fell motionless to the floor. Deacon felt the hole in his pants and raised the club to inflict punishment on the helpless dog.

"You leave Buster alone," screamed Sundra. Instinctively she grabbed the straw broom leaning against the wall and walloped Deacon over the head with it. "You should be ashamed," she stammered reproachfully.

"Lousy lil' furball should be tied up an' drowned fer snappin' me," spat Deacon, making no excuses or apologies as he stomped away from her sight.

With gentle fingers running over his back and legs, Sundra examined Buster and was relieved he wasn't seriously injured. He whined, and his tail started to wag when he sniffed the ham Sundra was offering him. The dog gobbled it up and licked his chops in gratitude, making Sundra smile.

She didn't like the idea of staying near the storeroom to play with Buster. What if Deacon should return, or worse, tell the duke about her unladylike actions and that she had no chaperone?

With Buster cuddled in her arms, Sundra turned to take him back to her cabin. There stood the duke, silent and forboding, directing a raised eyebrow at her behavior.

"Your Grace," whispered Sundra, suddenly feeling as though she had just been caught poaching.

"Leave him," demanded Gardner.

Sundra bit her lip and shooed away the dog. She squared her shoulders. So it had come down to this, had it?

"I thought Buster's affections were not included on my precious little list," she said dryly. "Heaven forbid that I should feel the need to seek out the companionship of a dog. Good day, Your Grace!"

Gardner nodded in satisfaction, which made the fire in her eyes flare in defiance. Before Sundra could take two steps away, she was swept off her feet, his muscled arms crushing her against his lean body.

His kiss was hard and very demanding, making her pulse quicken and race wildly out of control. She panicked when she felt the heat from his hand as it slowly moved up her back, clasping and kneading the soft tumbled curls at the nape of her neck.

As Sundra fought for breath, a thrilling numbness coursed through her veins. She wasn't aware Gardner had set her down until the nearness of his eyes staring into hers shocked her back to reality.

Lowering his head, Gardner took her lips with his, gently at first and then with a tender urgency which made Sundra quiver as she had done after their first passionate embrace at the chapel. A low chuckle snapped in her ears. The duke had dominated her without using force!

"I hate you!" she cried in shame. How could she have let herself succumb to his desires, knowing he didn't love her? Just because the duke might think he owned her, she was not about to let him trifle with her affections.

Gardner did not see the hot tears of anguish as she raced back to her quarters.

"Damn," he drawled. Sundra was a puzzle to him. One minute he could look into her sea-green eyes and see her soul begging to be trusted. Yet, she hadn't the evidence to discredit the entrapment scheme he'd accused her of. James believed her story. Why couldn't he? He certainly wasn't getting any answers from Lady Miriam either. Why, the woman was living like a hermit!

"Damn it to hell! She's got me talking to myself," swore Gardner. Sundra didn't deserve an explanation about the dowry or Alice, not after she caused a rift in his friendship with James. They could barely stand being in the same room together, arguing over her word against his!

"Companionship of a dog, indeed! Potts! Mr. Potts," he bellowed, hellbent on shouting down the walls as he summoned the cook.

Sundra sulked in her room all day and was thankful Coralee hadn't come in to disturb her. Besides, she wasn't prepared to answer why the duke made her feel unnerved because she didn't know why herself.

When she felt she had sat by the bay window long enough she got up, stretched, and moved around the cabin. It was filled with many interesting nautical instruments and charts, all neatly placed among the fine silks, costly decorations, and elegant furniture. It was nothing like the way she had imagined a captain's quarters. It was better suited for royalty, then quickly dismissed the idea because it made her think about the duke.

As Sundra was lighting the lanterns, Coralee came rushing into the room with flushed cheeks and the aroma of raspberry tarts following in her wake.

"Oh, your ladyship!" Coralee panted. "You've gone and done it now!"

Sundra made her come away from the door. "You scared me half to death running in here like that," she half-laughingly told her maid. "What's this 'your ladyship' talk? You know we are friends and that I want you to call me Sunny."

"You can tell that to His Grace over dinner tonight!"

Coralee wiped her forehead and looked to see what needed straightening before his lordship came to call.

"He's coming here?" exclaimed Sundra, demanding an explanation.

"I was having tea with Mr. Potts when His Grace burst into the galley and ordered us to start cooking and baking his favorite dishes for tonight, or else! Lucky for the cook that I know how to prepare a decent meal, otherwise he'd be late with dinner and I wouldn't want to face the duke no matter what, judging by the mood you put him in. His Grace was angry, as you well know, sayin' as how you wanted a dog's company and that you were going to have it, too! Oh, Sunny, you didn't call His Grace a dog, did you?"

"Certainly not!" Sundra defended herself.

"That dress will never do," admonished Coralee, eying the dull tweed frock that Sundra usually wore at home. "His Grace will be here any minute!"

Reluctantly Sundra changed into a gown and discouraged Coralee from fussing over her appearance. She caught herself trembling while she sat in the shadows—waiting. As Coralee passed by, she swiftly dabbed scented water on Sundra's neck, which annoyed if not frightened her all the more.

Mr. Potts appeared out of nowhere and set the table with linen and the best of china and crystal. Silver trays laden with covered dishes were placed on the sideboard.

Sundra frowned when her maid and the cook placed serving spoons and forks alongside each entree before they darted away. The buffet meant she was to dine with her husband—alone!

The duke arrived promptly at eight o'clock, dashingly handsome and arrogant as ever. Sundra remembered he had the same look about him when she chanced to meet him with Alice in London. The thought pained her to remember.

After his curt greeting the duke payed no mind to small talk and busied himself by filling their plates with crustacean delicacies.

Gardner glanced at Sundra and, raising an eyebrow, stared briefly at the untouched lobster in front of her. She forced herself to eat, fearing his glance was a command. Was there anything he did not notice?

Sundra enjoyed the excellent cuisine, partly because Gardner didn't dominate the scene with rage and she hadn't realized how hungry she really was. She permitted the duke to fill her glass with champagne, her first taste ever.

By the time dinner was concluded their pleasantries had turned into a flowing conversation which did not even hint at the tension between them. An undeclared truce prevailed.

"So, you like dogs and children," began Gardner, throwing down his lace cravat while he made himself comfortable. "What else?"

Sundra cleared the table by force of habit, contemplating his question. Gardner certainly wasn't giving her a plausible cause to argue, so far.

Without mentioning the Wellses or the foundling home by name, she talked about her life in the country. It was easy to speak about her simple pleasures, knowing she didn't have to face him while she lingered at the sideboard. She babbled excitedly how the first breath of spring would make her feel eager to see the buttercups and daffodils grace the woodland meadows. She loved to go barefoot in a clover patch and confessed she could daydream for hours beside a brook.

Sundra's enthusiasm for nature persuaded Gardner to speak about Canada. She could hardly wait to see the giant fir trees he described to her and the creatures of the forest she had known only through books. It never occurred to her that this forest surrounded her new home, or that she was being forced to live there against her wishes.

During the conversation Gardner wandered over to the bed and propped himself into a relaxed position. Sundra payed no mind; after all, this was his cabin. She would gladly settle for another room if he were to ask, but she was afraid to bring up the subject of sleeping arrangements.

Gardner gave Sundra as much attention as he did to the bottles of champagne, which he consumed entirely on his own, making her a trifle nervous whenever their eyes met across the room.

Sundra knew the hour was late when a soft yawn escaped her lips. She hoped the duke did not notice. She peeked shyly in his direction, her eyes suddenly flying wide open. Indeed he hadn't noticed—because he was fast asleep on her bed!

She ran to his side, but approached him with caution.

"Psst, Your Grace, wake up," she pleaded. "It is very late and I must ask you to leave."

To her astonishment, Gardner cracked a thin smile across his face which was beginning to shadow with tomorrow's growth of beard.

"Not yet," he requested in an easy manner. "There is something I must tell you . . . I . . ." he whispered, letting the words drift into silence.

Sundra studied his face and wondered if he'd had too much wine. Was he about to ask for assistance to get back to his own cabin—wherever that might be?

Frantically she searched the cabin. Her eyes rested on a large pitcher on the commode and she contemplated pouring the cold water over the duke's head. She was willing to do anything at the moment if it meant getting him out of her bed.

"Come closer to me, Sundra . . ." moaned Gardner.

What is the matter with him she thought, suddenly worried he might be ill and in need of attention. If she wasn't attending to his needs, then she would be blamed if something drastic were to happen to him.

She leaned over to check his condition and tugged at his sleeve. Nothing! He didn't move a muscle. Was he breathing or not?

Just when a lock of her hair brushed his cheek he sprang to life, wrapping his arms around her tiny waist. He pulled her into bed with him, holding her firm and snug.

Sundra froze, scarcely breathing while Gardner lazily entwined her hair with his fingers and gently nuzzled the softness of her neck.

"I want you, my innocent," he whispered huskily, taking a deep breath of her flowery scent.

"I don't belong here," Sundra protested in a quivering voice. Cautiously she tried to lift his arm away from her waist, only to feel his hand clamp down more possessively.

"Oh no you don't," he said with determination. "I mean to have you and there's no escaping me now." He sighed contentedly, having forcefully nestled her in the pillows beside him.

The gentle rocking of the ship and the champagne she'd drank with dinner made Sundra relax beside Gardner even though she knew she shouldn't. She didn't need a quilt to take away the chill, wondering what the duke would think of her if he knew she didn't mind the warmth his body offered hers.

If only she knew where her ignorance was leading her. Was it wrong of her to act in such a brazen manner when she had already accepted the security of his arms? Sundra did not know if she should oblige him, or even how to, and pondered the thought of resistance.

She felt the heat lingering on her shoulders from his lips, awakening a quivering, exhilarating sensation that quickened her pulse. She allowed Gardner to hold her intimately and, against her better judgment, heeded his soothing words of encouragement and guidance.

Their spirits drifted upward among the stars as he gently persuaded her to sample love's delights; a sacred passion shared between a man and wife. Minutes turned into hours—midnight into morning.

Without warning, a blast of frigid air shattered Sundra's blissful slumber and she plummeted back to reality, clutching the coverlet for protection. The instant she opened her eyes, the duke cast her a sheepish grin when she realized she was pressed against his body, and had been holding onto him for quite some time.

What had she done! How had she behaved? Sundra wished she could run away and hide, but knew it wouldn't change matters. The marriage had been consummated.

To add to her embarrassment, Coralee had entered the cabin

carrying her breakfast tray and had discovered her and the duke sharing a bed.

"Beg . . . beggin' your pardon uh, Your Grace," stammered Coralee. "I was surprised to see, I mean . . . I didn't think you'd be, er . . . I'll be back whenever her ladyship wishes," she mumbled, stretching her arm to push the tray to the center of the table because she was afraid to move closer to the bed. When she left, the frosty draft which had awakened Sundra was shut out as the door banged closed.

"Sharing your bed with me wasn't all that bad, now was it?" Gardner asked nonchalantly. He rolled out of bed, stretched his lean, naked body as he stood before the commode to dress. He looked into the mirror and caught a glimpse of Sundra's reflection. Her eyes were wide and her mouth hung open.

"Are you going to stay abed all day, or do I have to shake your little rump out of the ticking?"

As Sundra hurriedly threw back the covers she let out a squeal of embarrassment, realizing her own nudity. She hastily donned a chemise and flew across the room.

"I never meant for you to do . . . anything!" Sundra sputtered, only to receive an unabashed smile from her husband.

"No m'lady," he replied smugly, "you were never meant to play the ice maiden, no matter how much you profess to be one," amused to watch her blushing profusely. "I am certain if your simpering maid hadn't disturbed us, you would've had a hard time convincing me otherwise. As I recall," he added, flashing her a dazzling smile, "I wasn't the only one this morning making advances, as innocent as they were."

"Oh!" Sundra screamed in exasperation, ready to pull her hair in a fit of temper. "How dare you make insinuations!"

Someone began pounding the door. Gardner bade the visitor to enter before Sundra could stop him. When James traipsed inside, Sundra wished she could blend in with the woodwork.

"Good morning, Duchess," James said merely as an afterthought, appraising the duke with a speculative glance. "I was beginning to think you'd fallen overboard . . . Have you?" he mused, a twinkle in his eye.

"Sorry to disappoint you, James," said Gardner, a touch of irony in his cold voice. "Whatever brought you barging in here had damn well better be worthwhile. As you can see," he said, buttoning his rumpled shirt, "I'm not in the mood for early morning socials!"

"So I've gathered," James replied curtly. "Tobey spied a ship bearing down on us from the north. It may be too early to tell, but I suspicion it's the ship returning to England that we've been waiting for."

Sundra listened intently. She knew the mystery ship must be the reason why the *Northwind* had stood at anchor for days. Something was about to happen and she shivered when she heard that the gunners had been ordered to their stations.

"James, you're too damn competent, but I admire you all the same," the duke said, in his own way of thanking his friend. "But I warn you, let any man step out of line and you'll be dealt with severely. I want a peaceful boarding so they won't mistake us for privateers! Otherwise, I won't be able to question the captain about Alice's well-being."

Gardner and James started for the door but Sundra's scream stopped them from leaving. She had raced after them and, as they turned around, she unleashed her fury at close range.

"Alice?" Sundra shouted in disbelief. "You're concerned about Alice? What have I done, Your Grace," she asked shortly, "to deserve this? Haven't I suffered enough without you wanting to flaunt her in front of my face?"

"Oh, for Christ's sake," retorted Gardner. "Pay her no mind, James! She doesn't know about Alice and I don't have the time nor the patience to explain it all now. Trust me."

James merely shrugged his shoulders.

"How dare you scheme together!" stormed Sundra, throwing a book at them to vent her anger. It missed.

"Both of you are despicable," she hissed and this time picked up a vase and sent it crashing above their heads.

Gardner and James ducked, suddenly finding themselves chuckling at her poor aim.

Instead of barbs, Sundra started flinging the contents on the shelf at her guffawing targets. The men tumbled out and closed the door just in time to hear a water pitcher and basin smash against it.

Sundra threw herself down on the bed and wept into the pillow. Coralee returned and spent several hours trying to engage her in idle conversation while she tidied the cabin. Suddenly the atmosphere exploded with cannon fire, making the ship's planks vibrate and moan.

"Oh, lordy, Sunny! Git away from that window," cried Coralee, straining her neck from behind the alcove long enough to warn her mistress about her dangerous folly before she herself ducked back to safety.

Although the blasts from the cannons hadn't sounded out for fifteen minutes, it wasn't until Sundra scolded her maid that she finally dared to budge from her hiding place.

"No one's going to shoot you, Coralee! Please, won't you go and find out what has happened?" nudged Sundra.

The motion of the ship increased in rollicking magnitude with each minute Sundra waited for Coralee to return. If the disturbance continued she knew the maid would never make it back on her own accord—Coralee was prone to seasickness.

With a glum expression on her face, Sundra lit the hanging lanterns, keeping each one from swaying on the iron brackets until she could replace the globe securely over the burning wicks.

A supper tray was brought in for her shortly after sundown. Deacon remained mute to her questions, casting a long queried look at her figure illuminated by the candlelight.

"I think you had better leave," warned Sundra uneasily.

"She's absolutely right!" announced Miriam, strolling into the cabin with a pocket pistol pointed at the crude seaman. "If you so much as look at Lady Sundra, you'll have to answer to His Grace! Now then, you get the blazes out and stay clear!"

After Deacon stomped outside, Miriam bolted the door, replacing the gun inside her pocket. Sundra remained speechless, just as Miriam knew she would.

"How heartless of you to leave me at the mercy of the street-runners," snapped Miriam. "We wouldn't have a care in the world if only you had wed that dolt Elliot, and then taken the money and run! But no! You left me penniless, and alone, to face Elliot's wrath."

"Now just a minute," argued Sundra, none too surprised that Miriam had somehow caught up to her. "I know all about your tryst with Elliot Spencer! I was forced to secretly marry the duke because I was afraid of what you'd do to me."

"Oh, Sunny! Elliot was being nothing more than melodramatic," replied Miriam, sampling the cold meat tray. "Was it so wrong of me to want to share the St. Ives dowry without your knowledge?"

"Had you asked, I would have given it to you, if it would have spared my father a tortured mind before he died. You'll never know the trouble you've caused."

"Giles died of natural causes, you can't deny that, Sundra." Miriam sighed heavily. "I didn't think you'd understand my fear of debtors prison. At least your husband is worthy of sympathy by allowing me to flee England."

"Had he known the circumstances, I doubt if he would have offered you a place with us."

"I've refused his generous offer to house a poor relative," scoffed Miriam. "I'll reside with acquaintances in Fort Amherstburg. Provided, of course, that you'll give me an ample sum to start anew in life. Otherwise, I'll have no choice but to tag along on your honeymoon and force myself to live in your home."

Sundra turned away, her body racked with sobs as huge tears gushed down her reddened cheeks. "Why are you doing this to me?"

"Oh, stop that sniveling," ordered Miriam. "Do you think I want to hang around your dull little neck? Share the family money, Sundra, and I promise to make good. We'll be apart from each other! Please . . . I'm begging you!"

"All right! . . . I'll see what I can do for you," conceded Sundra.

"You won't regret it," declared Miriam, her skirt swishing as she sashayed to the door. "By the way, His Grace was so relieved to hear that his precious Alice had arrived safely in Canada that he saluted the other captain with a rousing volley!"

For days Gardner had ignored Sundra, leaving her dejected heart to fight an emotional battle. She mustered her courage and took James into her confidence before they would arrive in Canada on the following day.

"I've done nothing to hurt Gardner, and yet, he's trying to rub my nose in his affair with Alice. If he hates me this much, then why doesn't he give me an annulment?"

"Come sit with me," asked James, guiding her to the settee. "I will not allow you to embarrass yourself like this. I daresay 'tis not my place to be the one to offer an explanation, but you must be told the truth. Alice is Gardner's sister."

"What!"

"Let me finish," he protested softly. "Gardner ended his—er—friendship, with Alice Rose Hawthorne on the very day that you ran into him in London. You've confused her with Gardner's sister, who's also named Alice," James continued slowly. "I apologize for the duke. He's been troubled financially, and worried so much about his sister's safety that he didn't take the time to make any explanations."

"So!" pouted Sundra. "He married me for my dowry, and has amused himself with the way I've been carrying on? Oh, James!"

"I'm sorry if Gardner has hurt you," James said thoughtfully. "May I be frank with you, Lady Sundra?"

"Yes," she replied seriously.

"Since Gardner's made good his marriage, I'm afraid you've no grounds to successfully win an annulment on your own accord. A divorce is out of the question, you realize, although I may be able to help you with a separation, if you so wish. You've been treated poorly," he said regretfully, "and I, for one, believe that you are entitled to your freedom. Gardner's been his own man for so long, he'd be quite a ruthless rake for a woman of your gentle breeding to live with him."

"No!" Sundra suddenly protested. "I owe my life to His

Grace . . . no matter what he thinks of me. Perhaps 'tis high time someone teaches him that he can't change other person's lives without getting emotionally involved!"

"If anyone can rekindle Gardner's heartfelt trust in women again, 'tis you! Even his sister struck a cruel blow by running off to marry Charles Hewett without His Grace's consent. Needless to say, he's totally reconciled with his brother-in-law, yet he thinks he's failed Alice in some way and to make up for it, he's quite obsessed with providing his unneeded guardianship! I daresay Gardner is too high-spirited. You'll have my sympathy if you stay with him, so help me!"

"And I daresay Gardner doesn't realize that he'll have his hands full with an equally high-spirited wife as well," she said with a determined smile.

CHAPTER 7

Charles Hewett sat in his carriage parked on top of the hill, overlooking the navy yard at Amherstburg. For over an hour he watched with satisfaction the confusion that usually took place whenever a ship came into port.

Sailors and idlers raced up and down the gangplank. Men in coarse linen shirts, soaked with perspiration, heaved bundles of cotton goods tied with rugged twine. Cumbersome wooden crates littered the area pell-mell. Drivers shouted and cursed because they were forced to maneuver a crooked path in order to pass through the cluttered dockside.

In the midst of the hullaballoo stood Alice Foxworthy Hewett. Her exhausted state grew more apparent by the minute. She felt frazzled, rendered helpless against the continuous gusts of wind taking toll of her usually impeccable coiffure. A throng of illiterate seamen had tried to help her locate the person she was to meet, without success. In final desperation, she started shaking her ruffled parasol in the air, hoping to catch the attention of someone in authority.

It was time for Charles to descend the mount. He'd made Alice wait alone long enough. The team was eager to bolt ahead after standing idle for hours on the knoll. Charles called to Alice along the way. He knew his voice would be lost in the din, but it was a good gesture on his part.

"Alice, my love," he cheered, alighting from his seat. "Welcome to your new home! Oh my, but I've missed you!"

Hewett kissed his wife's cheek. Her eyes were wide and dewy. She melted against him.

"Oh, Charles," she whimpered, "for a moment I thought you'd never come, that you never received word I would be arriving today."

"Not on your life! Why, the minute I heard you were here, I whipped the horses all the way over from the fort! Er, 'tis good to see you again my love, but you look so pale. Is something troubling you?" he asked innocently, as if he didn't already know!

Alice covered her face with gloved hands, quickly nodding her head to answer yes. Charles grasped her by the arm. He forced himself to look amidst the crowd.

"Where the devil is Gardner? He should know better than to leave you standing alone in a place like this!"

"He didn't come with me," she sobbed. "He was called away at the last minute on urgent business. I received a message informing me to travel ahead without him. By then, I had waited so long for him to return that I thought I was going to miss my ship. I was upset, Charles, and I left the port authority building without waiting for the footman to come with me. That's when those men . . . tried . . . to . . . ."

Immediately Charles ushered Alice to the carriage. He started the horses off at a slow walk and headed toward his homestead beyond the edge of town. His patience was taxed from a rough night of unprofitable gambling, and he certainly didn't wish to hear Alice whimpering in his ears along the way.

"Something dreadful must have happened, otherwise you wouldn't be shaking like a leaf just thinking about it! You may as well tell me what sort of trouble your brother let you in for by deserting you on such short notice."

"Charles, please! 'Tis all my fault for not watching where I was going. I ran into a group of men who were loitering near the ship. They stole my crested ring, and if the captain hadn't been on deck and seen what was happening, I would have been beaten for the rest of my valuables. I wasn't hurt, Charles, but I was scared out of my wits and have been ever since," she wailed, twisting uncomfortably in her seat.

Charles leaned over and placed a kiss on the blade of her shoulder, pretending to be concerned over a handful of unruly reins. "I'm sorry you've had to go through such a harrowing experience. Lean on me and rest. You're safe now that I'm here."

"But, you haven't asked me about the baby!"

"You . . . miscarried?"

"No, silly! I only wanted you to know I didn't let anything happen to it, no matter what I've been through to get here," she said proudly.

Charles intentionally let the reins slip through his fingers, bending so low to retrieve them that Alice couldn't notice his disappointed frown.

"Now, Alice, please don't be offended, especially since we haven't seen each other in months, but you look absolutely dreadful! You worry me to no end."

"I'm tired, but that's to be expected after spending weeks crossing the ocean. I'll be fine, darling."

"A man who loves his wife as much as I do can't be too cautious! No telling what sort of disease you can pick up at sea without realizing it. Honestly, love, you look sickly to me. Too pale for your own good! If you don't look any better in a few days, I'm going to send for the doctor," he declared, giving the horses a good smack on their rumps.

"You're frightening me," she gasped in alarm, catching hold of her side when the wagon hit a deep rut in the road and jarred her insides. She swayed in her seat.

"Maybe I have been overdoing it a bit. Hold onto me, Charles! I'm not feeling as well as I thought."

Charles rolled his eyes at the paltry log-built home, annoyed to hear Alice sighing contentedly at the sight of their humble abode. He managed to carry his wife inside and settled her in bed upstairs without further ado, promising to prepare a supper tray after she had rested.

Alone in the kitchen, Charles tore into a loaf of bread and ate it with slices of goat's-milk cheese. Sloppily he washed it down his throat with a pint of stale ale, belching as he shoved away from the table. "I should have known that Adrian Shaw would bungle the job," he growled, marching off to his study.

He unlocked the rolltop desk and withdrew a leather pouch from a secret drawer. He had paid a handsome price for the magic powder, just in case his plan went awry. "And it better not be wasted," he thought aloud. No child, born or unborn, was going to make him take a step backward in the line of inheriting the Foxworthy fortune. The devil take it! Alice should have been roughed up enough to miscarry on board ship. 'Twas why Gardner had been detained—just in case his fast actions would delay the miscarriage Charles wished to bring about.

As far as he was concerned, the duke was also living on borrowed time. If all went well, Alice would eventually follow Gardner to the grave and then, and only then, would he be the very next in line to inherit the Foxworthy empire. Charles left the room with a smile on his face.

Wearily, Alice ate a small bow of venison stew and half a corn cake. Although the tea had a very bitter aftertaste, she forced herself to drink the whole pot because Charles looked at wit's end if she didn't swallow more.

After Charles finished washing the dishes, he went outside and threw the soapy water on the weeds next to the back porch. His moccasin boots didn't make a sound as he traveled past the barn and entered the woods. He attended to his personal needs behind the bushes, allowing himself a few extra minutes to bathe in the stream. By the time he returned to the house he felt clean and refreshed.

During the evening, Alice came down with a sudden high fever. Charles pretended to brave the darkness outside and fetched countless buckets of cold well water. He applied cold compresses throughout the night. Bedcovers were tossed aside. Clinging nightgowns were often replaced with fresh, dry ones. The fever raged out of control, just as Charles had expected.

Somewhere in the distance a panther screamed. Branches and twigs snapped under the weight of elusive creatures prowling the forest. Alice was convinced the wolves howling nearby were stalking the homestead.

Charles assured her the "maw-in-gaw," one wolf or a sizable pack, would not enter a well-lit house. Alice made him shut the windows regardless.

Another pot of tea was brewed. Alice was parched with thirst, but could not keep any of the liquid down. Her stomach was cramped. The pains were increasing in intensity. Her muscles tightened round her waist every five minutes, leaving her short of breath and exhausted during the brief intervals before the spasms started all over again. It wasn't long before Charles noticed bloodstains on the sheet.

He went downstairs and boiled a couple of trussing sponges in a pot. After they had been purified, he squeezed out the hot water. Nothing must happen to Alice—yet, he thought. She was the key access to her brother's wealth and power. Acting like a midwife, Charles took the sponges, along with a pail, and walked briskly to the bedroom to finish his duty.

Dawn spread a gray blanket across Alice, who had finally fallen asleep, but with a troubled mind. Charles pulled down the shade and closed the drapes, retreating to the kitchen for a hearty breakfast—without so much as one regret over the night's outcome.

Charles's nerves were frayed after an exasperating week of listening to his wife wailing herself into a dither over the loss of the babe he never wanted in the first place. He didn't cotton to handholding and wasn't about to give Alice any cosseting words of comfort. No, sir! He was going to pack up his puffy-ankled, recently turned frigid wife and confront Gardner with his miserable lot. All he had to do was riddle the duke's conscience with guilt for causing his sister's sufferings. Charles's palms were itching as he thought about the goodly sum of restitution surely to come his way, and he would pressure Gardner to sign a valid will naming Alice as sole beneficiary. Just how soon Alice would sign it over to him was up to his impeccable discretion.

Alice was tossing in bed, softly calling out to her husband, who hadn't been listening. "Plain water," she begged, "not that awful brew you've been giving me. Please?"

"What's this!" sputtered Charles. "Now, Alice, my love, you've got to let other people help you. Lord knows I'll have enough on my hands when I go to see that brother of yours without having to worry about your health, too! . . . er, dear heart."

"But you implied I miscarried from catching some disease on the ship. 'Tis my fault for being careless, not Gardner's."

"Enough! I tell you the duke is the cause of this, and by hell, he's going to pay for what he's put us through. I'll horsewhip that rake within an inch of his fool life, I will!"

Alice's eyes grew wide with fear. She'd never seen Charles so upset, his good nature turned sour with intended violence. He certainly wasn't acting like the man she had married. Somehow she must bring peace between the two men she loved.

Turning to face Charles in the dim candlelight, she looked pleadingly into his eyes. "I'll do anything to renew the love and trust between you and my brother. I'll ask . . . no, I'll demand, that Gardner give me the best of care and the run of the manor, if only you'll let me go with you to Tamarack."

Charles raised an eyebrow. Alice had said the very words he wanted to hear.

"It would be better for you to have the duke's servants waiting on you hand and foot, since we haven't any," he contemplated out loud. "But what will people think of a husband who allows his wife to get out of her sickbed so soon? No, madam wife. It just wouldn't be proper."

Silently, Charles checked the time on his gold pocket watch, inwardly pleased that his wife had taken the bait.

"So be it," he conceded to Alice. "Your gentle ways have won me over. You've a right to your brother's luxuries and you had better keep your promise by demanding your share of attention. Bachelors like Gardner have to be told straight out. They don't know a woman's needs. Now mind that you get plenty of rest. We'll be leaving the day after the morrow."

Charles ordered his complaisant wife to stay safely abed while he left the house to attend urgent business. He reached the dockside tavern in record breaking time and settled down with a tankard of ale to wait.

Just as much as Charles was surefooted and walked with an air of dignity, Fishbait Gilly rambled about with bunioned feet, which made his unbalanced gait seem clumsy.

Gilly removed his oily stock cap, bobbed his head of matted hair, and told Charles another gentleman wished to speak with him outside. "By tha oook tree," he spit, holding out his hand for a shilling reward.

Charles merely gave Gilly a kick in the seat of his pants for his effort, and marched outside for his secret meeting.

"Dammit, Deacon! Where the deuce have you been? I heard the *Northwind* put in anchor at Tamarack days ago!"

"Ah, Hewett, still as friendly and patient as ever," Deacon replied ironically. "I'd feel a mite better if I had the remainder of my pay in me pockets before I loosen up me tongue for the likes of you."

Charles sputtered, "You were told to keep an eye on Shaw! Obviously you didn't, because I had to take care of Alice's condition myself!"

"You won't be so tightfisted when I tell you that I killed Shaw before your brother-in-law could beat the truth out of him," Deacon replied impatiently. "The villagers think Gardner's at fault."

Charles pondered the issue for a moment. "I suppose when the time is right, we could confront him with a murder charge. Ho ho, Deacon! I may be a lot richer sooner than I thought," boasted Charles, dangling a small pouch of gold for Deacon to take.

"Laugh all you want now, but you've the devil to face soon enough! I swear Gardner worried more about his sister's welfare than the bloody storms we fought at sea. He was livid when he heard Alice wasn't quickly escorted away from the Amherstburg docks."

"Then he'll be more than willing to compensate for Alice's misfortunes by the time I get done with him," guffawed Charles. "What more can a man ask?"

"Perhaps you'd better ask your little bit-o-lace and confidante, Miriam Bradford. She's staying with the Engmanns."

"Now why the blazes would she come here," scoffed Charles. "I told that woman I'd be sending for her soon enough!"

"Like it or not, Charlie," replied Deacon, "she ran away from her debts just as fast as Gardner captured her cousin for his wife. Her name be Sundra Foxworthy right and proper."

"What! Now see here! Don't you joke with me . . ."

"'Tis the truth! I've already given you more information than what you've paid for, you cheap bastard! I'm getting myself a drink," shouted Deacon, leaving Charles to stand alone in the cold.

"By all means, do!" snickered Charles, not caring if he'd ever see the likes of Deacon again. Without the ocean to keep them apart as beforehand, he was going to meet with his lovely Miriam, and together, with Alice to help serve their purpose, he fancied himself and his mistress fine masters of fate and fortune. One day soon my raven-haired beauty will share my upcoming empire and my bed, Charles mused.

CHAPTER 8

Tamarack estate had overwhelmed Sundra's wildest imagination. The imposing thirty-room manor, complete with gatehouse and white picket fences and uniformed servants, had welcomed her with all the pomp and circumstance befitting a new duchess' homecoming. Yet in all the elegant surroundings she remained a country lass at heart. It was as though the very brim of wilderness inspired her to be herself.

Sundra bounced out of bed at the crack of dawn, pausing for a moment to chase away the shivers while she washed in her rose-pink bedchamber. Quickly she dressed in a fine kersey wool gown laid out the night before in anticipation of joining her elusive husband for breakfast in the morning room.

After racing down the winding staircase at breakneck speed, she stopped in the mirrored hallway to smooth her skirt and tumbled curls. She was anxious to catch Gardner before he went riding off to the fields, but equally concerned she didn't appear to have run like the devil in getting there.

In response to her exasperated sigh, the door to the cozy room swung open while Sundra was straightening a ribbon. A plump hand reached out, pulling her like a tottering child across the threshold.

"I was just tellin' His Grace wot a foin mornin' it be," chortled Mrs. McDewey, prodding Sundra to take a seat next to the duke, who acknowledged her with a curt nod.

Gardner resumed staring out the window while he drained the last of his tea. "I don't have time for breakfast, McDewey," he suddenly announced. "Have lunch sent to the south gate around noontime." He pushed away from the table without giving Sundra a second glance, threw his napkin on the chair, and walked over to the coat rack.

"Where the devil is my riding crop!"

"Oh, I'll get it . . . I'll get it," puffed Mrs. McDewey, giving him a cold stare before she stomped out of the room. She couldn't help but notice the disappointed frown on Sundra's face. His Grace couldn't have brought home a sweeter wife, she thought, and yet it was obvious he didn't want to spend the time of day with her.

With a smile Sundra stood up and covered her shoulders with a knitted cloak. The duke turned around just as she was nearing the door. He was scowling.

"And where, may I ask, do you think you're going?" snapped Gardner impatiently.

"With you," Sundra replied casually. "I thought perhaps you'd give me a tour of the estate."

"Everyone at Tamarack has work to do, madam," he said curtly, "and your job is to run the household according to my expectations. I should think you'd enjoy accounting for the silver and crystal without wanting to frolic in the wildwoods."

"I only wanted to go out . . ."

"None the less," the duke interrupted rudely, "you'll either get lost or be in the way!"

"I see," whispered Sundra, her eyes filling with tears.

As Gardner slammed the door behind him, Sundra trudged back to the solitude of her room. She had had every hope and intention of becoming friends with him—if nothing else. She had been mistaken in thinking his aloof attitude toward her would change once they had settled in Canada. Gardner was keeping his distance, holding her to a promise of being his wife in name only.

"There you are, Sunny," cried Coralee, happily floundering in the midst of ruffles and lace. "Us being here's like a dream, eh? Oohh, wot ye look at this," she squealed with delight. She dived her hands into the trunk and came up with an armful of fluffy chemises.

"Those aren't mine," Sundra said shaking her head, "and I certainly didn't order anything when we stopped in Quebec."

"His Grace said you needed a complete trousseau," Coralee

stated as a matter of fact. "Don't look so surprised! That wee box you brought along can't hold enough clothes to keep ye warm through the winter, much less clothe ye in all the proper attire befitting a lady of yer station, now, will it?"

As if I care, thought Sundra. Puzzled, she took the wrapped box from Coralee and opened it. She fingered the blue negligee and miniature rosettes which Addie had created during alterations. She closed her eyes and heard the haunting memory of an intimate whisper beckoning to her: "You would look far lovelier in that negligee than Alice Rose," the arrogant stranger had once told her.

No less, she had married that arrogant man and, with a mischievous glint in her eye, she wondered if the same gown would be tempting enough to make her husband squirm and regret his decision to keep a wife in name only.

"Coralee, is there a riding habit in that trunk?"

"Yes'm," replied Coralee.

"Fine! Please get it ready for me," Sundra bade her politely, and hurried to slip out of her plain woolen gown.

Armed with an encouraging slap on the back from Mrs. McDewey and a hamper crammed with food, Sundra went riding along an oak-lined path which should have led her to the south gate twenty minutes ago.

Just as it seemed to Sundra that she had traveled for miles, the chestnut horse finally stopped in a clearing and pulled on the reins in order to nip at the scraggy clumps of grass.

The field area appeared deserted and Sundra silently pondered her next move. Suddenly, a chopping noise arose from a nearby grove of aspen and pine. The horse pricked his ears, snorted, and suddenly reared back. The food hamper opened and the contents scattered in all directions.

"Timberrr . . ."

A giant fir tree moaned overhead, tearing away branches from neighboring trees as it crashed to earth with a thunderous roar.

The ground trembled, and the skittish horse bucked, throwing Sundra into a clump of thistles. The wind carried shouts from the forest after she had screamed, and soon a rider was bearing down the path toward her.

"Oh no! Stop! You'll ruin your lunch," Sundra cried in vain. Horrified, she watched Gardner dismount and step on the roast fowl that was to have been his meal. The loaf of bread and the frosted maple cake had been trampled on by his horse.

"Are you hurt?" bellowed Gardner.

Embarrassed, Sundra shook her head no.

After a silent ride on the back of Gardner's horse, Sundra was deposited none too gently on Mrs. McDewey's doorstep.

Mrs. McDewey took Sundra under her wing and gave her a tour of the lower levels and underground rooms at Tamarack. The cellar chamber stored huge blocks of ice nestled between layers of clean straw. Handsaws displaying jagged edges hung from the rafters; hand-forged tools which the workmen had used during the winter to cut frozen chunks from nearby Lake Erie.

Sundra made a point of acquainting herself with the staff and thanked them for making her feel welcome at Tamarack.

"And you, Evans, have done a splendid job keeping order during these past hectic days," she commented, nodding graciously at the butler, who was, and always had been, the major-domo of all the Foxworthy residences.

"Thank you, your ladyship," Evans replied in a nasal drawl, never cracking a smile on his stolid face.

A hearty roast-beef dinner was sent to Sundra's room. She didn't touch it, but promised to order a cup of tea before the cook retired for the night. Coralee appeared and peeked at her from the doorway.

"Psst! I've brought ye a friend," whispered Coralee.

"Buster!"

The terrier pranced across the hardwood floor and spun around in circles until Sundra scooped him up in her arms. All night they kept each other company while Sundra read until the darkness turned into dawn.

Late in the morning, with Buster nipping at her heels, Sundra headed for the study to apologize for ruining the duke's favorite lunch. Gardner's growling commands could be heard coming from behind the closed door, sending Evans and pages scurrying out to do his bidding.

"Oh, Evans," called Sundra. "Would you please tell His Grace that I wish to speak with him?"

Evans peered down his aquiline nose. "I'm terribly sorry, your ladyship. His Grace shouldn't be disturbed right now. You see, Dr. Todd is with him at the moment."

"He's ill?" she gasped.

Before the butler could convince Sundra otherwise, she impulsively opened the door and dashed inside the study. Judging by the startled expression on Dr. Todd's face and the penetrating scowl on Gardner's, Sundra suddenly had the sinking feeling of having rudely interrupted them.

"Ah, Lady Sundra," greeted Dr. Todd. " 'Tis a pleasure to see you again. I'm afraid I've monopolized His Grace's time by going over this medical inventory. Do hope you don't mind."

Oh dear, thought Sundra, looking at an assortment of glass vials and pill boxes littering the top of Gardner's mahogany desk. "I didn't mean to intrude," she whispered. "If you'll excuse me, gentlemen, I'll leave you to business."

"Yes, do," Gardner replied coldly.

As Sundra grabbed hold of the ivory doorhandle, she heard the doctor gasp out loud.

"Good heavens," retorted Dr. Todd. "Where did that mongrel come from?"

The physician turned, cradling a long-haired cat in his arms. Both were looking spellbound at the terrier quietly stalking toward them.

With hackles raised, Buster lunged full speed ahead and attacked the doctor's trousers in an attempt to reach the furry enemy.

Hissing, the cat clawed away from the doctor, blundering across the desk before climbing the bookshelf for safety. Buster followed in hot pursuit. The remainder of toppled vials went crashing to the floor. The cat could not find refuge on the narrow ledges and, with claws extended, made a daring leap for the satin draperies.

After everyone had retired that night, Sundra tiptoed back to the study with Coralee's sewing basket. While she was stitching she wondered what fate had befallen Buster. Either the loyal staff didn't know, or they were reluctant to tell her.

"Should ye be doing that?" asked Mrs. McDewey as she came up behind Sundra.

"Considering all the trouble I've caused, 'tis the least I can do," Sundra replied sincerely. "I'm truly sorry."

Sundra's glum expression and lack of spirit worried the woman.

"Ye've dun naught wrong, lassie," Mrs. McDewey spoke softly, "'cept to luv a man who's not prepared to luv ye back until he comes to grips with hisself."

"I don't think Gardner trusts or even wants me."

Mrs. McDewey clucked her tongue. "Hah! Yer a foin, rare woman, Sundra Foxworthy, and well he knows it! Give His Grace time to put his life in order. Heaven knows he'll need someone like you by his side after Mr. Hewett gits through with him."

"Do you know when he's coming?" asked Sundra in concern.

"No," Mrs. McDewey said, shaking her head, "but the fires in hell'll be burnin' bright the day he comes."

After a sleepless night, Sundra hid in the solarium while waiting for Gardner to leave the breakfast room. She then cautiously darted past a deserted pantry and ran down the short flight of stairs, entering the brick-walled tunnel leading to the cookhouse.

Maggie and a scullion boy stopped and smiled at her, adjusting a rack of fresh smoked sausage on their shoulders.

"Mornin', your ladyship," they chanted.

Sundra gave them a friendly nod as she paused to catch her breath. "Maggie, did you happen to see a small dog anywhere near the manor?"

The woman shook her head no.

"I did," replied Kip in an energetic voice. "The gamekeeper took him out to Point Pelee yesterday, but the dog wasn't with him when he came back this mornin'. Plenty o' ducks in the marsh this time o' year to keep the rascal busy if he runned off the handlers leash, I suppose."

"Is the Point very far away?" asked Sundra.

"No'm. Ye goes past the south gate, head west and follow the shoreline fer 'bout ten miles."

Unfortunately Sundra's horse went lame halfway to Point Pelee. Having had the experience of tending her own mount at the vicarage, she knew she hadn't the proper tools to remove the sharp pebble wedged between the hoof and shoe. She took off the saddle and decided the horse would be capable of returning to the stables without her help. She continued calling Buster's name, hoping to see the terrier charging to catch up to her at any minute.

After Sundra had walked through a dense patch of cattails, she cast aside her sodden shoes. Eventually her barefoot search led her to a long strip of sandy beach.

The sun warmed her body while she lay against a sand dune, avoiding the cool wind that was ever present. Overhead seagulls soared in the azure sky. Sundra felt free for the first time since she'd made Canada her home.

The sky would stay muted red for another short hour until nighttime descended over the countryside. Misty patches of frost were starting to cover the lowland meadows, plunging temperatures to chill the bone. There should have been a fire burning in the hearth inside the duke's study, but there wasn't. Instead, Coralee stood cowering behind Mrs. McDewey while both of them shivered. All too soon they heard His Grace striding into the damp room, letting out an exasperated sigh.

"Make it brief, McDewey," said Gardner grimly. "I'm needed back at the warming barns."

Coralee let out a wail, only to receive a jab in the ribs from Mrs. McDewey.

"Sunny's missing," blurted Coralee, heedless.

"Er, wot she means, Your Grace, is that Lady Sundra rode off to the Point, and hasn't returned home yet."

The duke narrowed his eyes as he glared at Mrs. McDewey's pale face. "You allowed her to go . . . alone?"

"I did nothing of the sort!" replied the woman. "Only an hour ago we missed her hereabouts. We started askin' fer her and learned she went off to find Buster. Kip told her the game-keeper took the dog to Point Pelee."

Gardner stiffened in astonishment at Sundra's folly. What-ever possessed her to think she could go traipsing off alone in the wilderness, unarmed and probably ill-clothed, he'd never know.

"Sound the warning bell, McDewey," Gardner ordered sharply, snatching a gun from the cabinet.

The men in the search party lit their torches before splitting up to ride off in different directions. Gardner spurred his horse once he reached the shoreline. He'd go straightaway to the Point while the others were scouring the southwestern trail just in case Sundra had wandered off the path.

The duke spied Sundra's castoff saddle in the brush and headed toward the west cranberry pond. As his horse forded a stretch of marshland, several white-tailed deer could be seen sprinting back to the woods.

Gardner dismounted on the beach, tying the reins to a sta-tionary piece of driftwood. Swiftly, before the shroud of dark-ness enveloped the area, he followed a trail of tiny footsteps imprinted in the white sand.

He heard Sundra crying long before he spied her in the evergrowing darkness. "Sundra!" he called in a deep voice, hearing her sobbing in response.

"Oh, Gardner," cried Sundra as she came rushing to throw her arms around him, desperately clinging to him with all her might.

"Are you all right?" he asked without relaxing his hold, thankful to have her back in his arms once again, his pride and arrogance forgotten.

Frozen in silence, they held each other momentarily while a canopy of stars was flickering overhead.

Candlelight was shining out of every window at Tamarack, welcoming the couple home as they rode into the frosty courtyard. The warning bell clanged once again to call back the other men. Evans stood erect between the baronial columns in the portico, stifling the faintest hint of a smile.

"I should slap your bottom for keeping the staff awake all night," teased Gardner as he escorted Sundra inside. He then carried her up the winding staircase leading to her room, only to be rerouted by Mrs. McDewey.

"She'll have a hot bath in here," ordered Mrs. McDewey, pushing open the door to Gardner's bedchamber. Next she nudged the duke back into the hallway, looking over her shoulder to make sure Coralee was attending to her mistress. "Git yerself a warm brandy, Master Gardner, and when yer dun, ye'll see to it that this lass stays warm all night!"

The duke raised an eyebrow at his old nurse, inwardly amused she should use the tone of voice he had come to regard with fondness during earlier days in the schoolroom. The nerve of that woman!

"Precisely what I had in mind, McDewey," he answered, "and I'll thank you to remember that it was I who made the decision."

Although Sundra felt comfortable beneath the weight of the feather ticking, she could not fall asleep; nor could she pretend to be when Gardner sauntered into the room an hour later.

"Feeling better?" he asked, offering her a mug of hot toddy. He paused, letting his eyes slowly wander down the length of her covered body. "I suppose I haven't made it easy for you to adjust to living here."

Sundra was temporarily speechless, wishing with all her heart that he genuinely cared for her. His change in attitude was too sudden and she felt ill at ease, thinking he was acting out of guilt. She was doubting his motives. Gardner had rescued her, held her safe and delivered her to a new home—all the things he had wanted to do for his sister Alice but failed to accomplish through no fault of his own.

"Don't," she said, brushing away his hand caressing her cheek. "I'm . . . sorry," she stammered. "It's just that I . . . don't want you to take pity on me or confuse me with someone else."

"After the ruthless way I've treated you, I can't blame you for doubting me," confessed Gardner. "Pride be damned, m'lady. I've tried to deny my true feelings ever since I laid eyes on you."

Sundra thought about Gardner's unpredictable temper, but gathered her courage to speak her mind anyway. "There've been too many misunderstandings between us. Nothing has been resolved and I still feel as though I'm nothing but a silly burden to you," she said decisively. "In fact, I shouldn't be here in your bed!"

Of course Sundra had been wishing for a breakthrough to Gardner's affections, but now she found herself fighting against the opportunity of a dream come true.

As Sundra jumped out of bed Gardner grabbed ahold of her shoulders. "Shall we sit and talk by the fire?" he asked in a threatening tone, forcing her into a chair unmindful of her protests. "Quite frankly madam, it's about time I took you in hand! If I don't, you and that dog and miserable cat, are liable to bring the roof down over our heads."

"Ohh!" fumed Sundra, her green eyes flaring with defiance. Like a flash she was up and facing him. "And I don't suppose you're ever going to let me forget about the lunch hamper either!"

"That is correct," grinned Gardner, "unless, of course, you promise to kiss me the next time I have to rescue your little rump from the marsh."

Suddenly Sundra's eyes grew misty, worrying about the dog still lost in the dangerous marsh and about having endangered Gardner's life when he had braved the darkened wildwoods to find her. Something drastic could have happened to him and she desperately wished to feel the comfort of her husband's arms around her.

Sensing a change, Gardner grasped her tightly to him, murmuring soft words as his mouth moved against her lips, eagerly pressing harder when she responded to his kiss. He felt her fingers caressing the back of his neck and wondered if she was aware that her touch was stimulating his desires.

"I once warned you that I would make a very demanding husband," Gardner whispered huskily, lifting her up into his arms and carrying her to the canopy bed. Stripped of his shirt, he lay next to her on the mattress, capturing and holding her lips as his hand untied the ribbons on her nightgown.

Sundra was pressed against his bare chest, her heart beating wildly against the hand that was fondling her, lost in amazement that her flesh was responding to his gentle kneading. Her eyes widened as he shed the last of his garments; she blushed at the boldness of their nudity which he took so calmly.

Aware of Sundra's inexperience and increasing reluctance, Gardner plied her with softened kisses, guiding her timorous hands to touch, and teaching her supple body how to respond to please him.

"Do not be afraid," he whispered in her ear, coaxing her fingertips to explore for the first time. "We will give each other great pleasures of love," he drawled heavily.

When they were comfortably settled beneath the quilt, Sundra gave in to the exhilarating sensation caused by their movements. Her mind was so completely dominated by sheer ecstasy, that she could find no words to describe the pleasure of their union.

With tears in her eyes, Sundra whispered his name while he lay breathing heavily beside her. "Do you truly love me," she asked softly.

"Love?" The duke lightly mocked her, a sheepish grin spreading across his flushed face. "Madam, need you ever ask?" He chuckled and pulled her closer, lavishing her lithe body with searing kisses. They made love throughout the night, experiencing heights of passion known only to them.

At noon, when Sundra had walked the quarter mile to bring him a lunch hamper, Gardner immediately set aside his work and found a secluded spot underneath an ancient oak tree for them to share.

"You look rather domesticated today," teased Gardner, giving her a kiss as he surmised her red checkered linen gown and long shawl. "I suppose I have McDewey to thank for this."

Sundra chuckled in earnest, happy she wasn't expected to dress in silks and sit idly about. "Actually, she was reluctant to let me wear this outside the cookhouse. I'm helping make jerky today, you know," she said proudly.

"Hmm," mumbled Gardner, attacking another slice of ham.

"Maggie says there'll be a lot of men to feed when they come to help transplant the tobacco next month."

The furious ringing of the warning bell interrupted their conversation. Gardner jumped to his feet as one of the workers hurried to lead the duke's horse into the clearing.

Sundra noticed the anxious frown on Gardner's face, knowing she would only slow him down if they rode back together. "You ride on ahead," offered Sundra. "I'll walk back with the others."

A strange assortment of wagons and drays were parked pell-mell in the courtyard. Sundra ran the length of the winding driveway and entered the manor through the opened portico doors. She rounded the corner and saw Evans closing the study door behind him. She could hear a stranger's angry voice coming from the room before the door was fully closed.

"Damn you, Gardner! 'Tis all your fault, as you well know!"

The butler leaned against the wall and, spying Sundra out of the corner of his eye, quickly regained his expressionless composure.

"Evans, what's going on here?" asked Sundra excitedly.

"By all that is holy, your ladyship, I beg of you not to disturb His Grace right now," Evans replied in a somber voice. "Please excuse me, m'lady," he said, abruptly rushing away.

Hiking up her skirt, Sundra took the stairs two steps at a time. When she reached the top she skidded to a halt.

Coralee, with tears streaming down her freckled cheeks, was on her hands and knees frantically trying to assemble the lot of Sundra's wardrobe which had been hastily dumped on the hallway floor.

"Who's responsible for this!" demanded Sundra.

Coralee stood up, motioning with her hands for Sundra to lower her voice. "I don't know," she whispered, absentmindedly wiping her nose on her dress sleeve. "There's a sick woman in there who looks as though she's on death's doorstep. Oh, Sunny, if we disturb her rest, we'll git a curse put on our bloomin' heads, I just know it!"

"Nonsense," hissed Sundra. "Where is Mrs. McDewey?"

Coralee jerked her thumb toward the bedchamber that Sundra and Gardner had shared last night. "She's been in there fer hours," she sniffed, "an' fer all I know, Mrs. McDewey could be lyin' dead on the floor by now! Oohhh . . ."

To keep Coralee from wailing into hysterics, Sundra had to pinch her on the arm, making her jump two feet off the floor.

Sundra's belongings were placed in the rose room she had originally occupied since she'd come to Tamarack. She hadn't the faintest idea where Gardner's clothes had been thrown or which bedchamber he was to occupy now that the mysterious lady had commandeered their nuptial suite. Everyone in the household had a supper tray sent to their rooms and, according to rumor, the duke had ordered absolute quiet for the night's duration.

Morning came and Sundra could stand no more lallygagging from the servants. No one smiled or offered explanations about the peculiar houseguest and disruptive changes in routines. She stormed downstairs where Evans rushed over to meet her.

"His Grace has asked to see you, your ladyship."

Gardner and the stranger stood up when Sundra entered the study. She skirted around the desk and stood defensively by her husband's side.

"Sundra, may I present my brother-in-law, Charles Hewett," Gardner stated wearily, the strain of a sleepless night shadowing his rugged face. "Charles, this is my wife, Sundra."

"How do you do," Sundra said softly.

Charles bowed and extended his arm, lightly touching her fingertips as he kissed her hand. He cocked his head to one side and gave Gardner a nod of approval, saying: "Now I can understand why you didn't waste time in marrying such a lovely lady. You always were the one who, shall we say, took the best advantages which life could offer? Well now," he said, kissing Sundra's hand again and clicking his heels together, "you must not think it rude of me for wanting to take my leave so soon after your arrival. I've been away from Alice's bedside far too long."

Sundra gasped in surprise. "I had no idea Lady Alice was the woman upstairs. But of course!" she added, noticing that Charles's eyes had darkened and narrowed when he witnessed her delayed reaction. "Is Alice . . . ill of health?" questioned Sundra, suddenly feeling apprehensive.

"We're not certain about her condition," replied Gardner, holding Sundra's eyes captive with a piercing, reproachful, gaze, ". . . until Dr. Todd returns from Montreal. Due to my negligence, she's suffered a miscarriage."

"The devil be hanged, Trentbay," Charles responded harshly. "How you could allow such an incompetent physician to remain in your employ is beyond my comprehension. You can see for yourself he's neglected his duties with the infirmary!"

"As I told you before, Charles," retorted the duke, "I take full responsibility for the loss of Dr. Todd's medical supplies. Until he returns, we'll just have to rely on McDewey's nursing abilities."

"Regardless of your faith in the old nanny, I still say Alice is in one hell of a predicament thanks to you, and well you know it," Charles snorted. He bowed stiffly, turned on his heel, and left the room.

"Oh, Gardner!" sighed Sundra, placing her arms around his neck, her elated smile somewhat dampened with guilt. "I can't tell you enough how sorry I am to have caused damage to Dr. Todd's supplies. But you know, Alice surely can't be too badly off if she managed to travel by wagon. Oh, I'll wager she was most happy to see you!"

"Happy?" exploded Gardner, shrugging off Sundra's embrace. "Madam, my own sister would not even acknowledge my presence in the room!"

Charles dismissed Mrs. McDewey for the duration of his visit with Alice. He strutted throughout the bedchamber, satisfied with the luxurious accommodations, and at his wife's behavior, for Alice wouldn't have settled for less, thanks to his persuasion.

"Oh, Charles," called Alice, patting the bed until he obeyed and sat down beside her. "Have you made peace with my brother?"

"You could say we've reached an agreement of sorts," he said cautiously, "although I must warn you that I was correct to assume he was the cause of your mishaps. He admitted his guilt and wants to make amends for having failed to deliver you safely to Canada. Knowing his pride, let him think he's got to earn back your love and trust," advised Charles.

So far so good, thought Charles, patronizing Alice by fussing with her lifeless hair while marveling at his ability to outwardly remain calm when his mind was in a quandary. The sudden shock of the duke's hasty marriage left a bitter taste in his mouth. The last thing he needed was a duchess obstructing the path to his inheritance!

"La, Charles," sang Alice, "I feel like a queen, the way you pamper me so. You know, I can't remember the last time Gardner took a personal interest in me. Oh, he's made certain that I've had the proper friends and schooling, but never did he allow me to interfere with his own life . . . until now. I rather enjoy taking matters into my own hands! 'Tis a power similar to that with which you mastered our elopement."

"You deserve the best, and well Gardner knows it. Not being a family man himself, why else would he have built Tamarack, if he didn't have the intentions of sharing it with his married sister? But I don't know what to think now, my love," rasped Charles, making a dramatic sweep across his beaded forehead.

"We're so close to becoming a united family, only to have more disheartening news which could hamper our reconciliation."

Alice stopped digging for a chocolate bonbon and folded her arms smugly across her chest. "Hmm. I thought something was amiss the moment we set foot in this house!"

Charles nodded in agreement. He watched her face pale when he broke the news of Gardner's marriage, adding his own untrue conclusions to make Alice suspect Sundra was a fortune hunter.

"You remember meeting her cousin, Lady Miriam, at the Engmanns' before we left Amherstburg? Well, she told me in so many words that the chit was not to be trusted!"

Alice began to weep into her scented pillow. "Poor Gardner," she sniffed. "What are we going to do?"

"I think your brother has doubts of his own concerning his marriage. Somehow we'll think of a way to help him," Charles egged her on, "but we must be very careful not to openly voice our suspicions while we live in the midst of the enemy."

Breakfast was the only time Sundra and Gardner could afford to spend together. With planting season four weeks away, the duke was busy making certain the tender shoots of tobacco were properly cared for in the hothouses if he hoped for a good crop come August. Cutting the best of solid oaks and pliant firs to supply the shipbuilders at the developing navy yard in Amherstburg filled the remainder of the duke's heavy work schedule.

Since Charles rarely left Alice's bedchamber in the days that followed, managing the business ledgers fell upon Sundra's shoulders—along with running errands for the Hewetts and secretly lending a hand to Maggie in the cookhouse.

On a frosty April morning Sundra stood within the circle of warmth from the open fire, laughing away lonely thoughts as she and Maggie struggled to keep Kip from falling into the kettle while he poured one hundred pounds of sal-soda into thirty gallons of soft water and stone lime. Another copper kettle held one hundred and twelve pounds of melting tallow to which Maggie had mixed fifty-six pounds of rosin and eight pounds of palm oil.

After the first kettle's mixture had boiled and settled, Kip poured off the lye and mixed the residue with the contents of the second kettle.

"This is the best yellow bar soap I've made yet," boasted Maggie, "and I couldn't have done it without yer help, m'lady."

Sundra smiled as she passed another flat box over the table for Maggie to fill. "It certainly is, Maggie, only I wish we could have made something more delicate for Lady Alice to use," she said hesitantly, thinking a small token would help ease the strain between her relationship with her sister-in-law. Charles had quickly befriended her, but Alice remained untouched by Sundra's kindness. But she didn't press the matter, realizing how the trauma of Alice's miscarriage could have affected her personality.

"I kin rightly turn out a batch o' transparent soap," offered Maggie, doling out molasses gingerbread after her job was done. "If Kip could sneak away a half gallon o' alcohol from the infirm'ry . . . and if . . . McDewey'll part with an ounce of sassafras essence. I know she ain't got much left this time o' year."

Sundra offered to gather a fresh supply of sassafras to replace Mrs. McDewey's supply and walked across the northern paddock to find the herb patch before it grew dark.

Tonight was the first time the family would dine together and, although Sundra didn't care that she had no say as to what was to be served, she was making every effort to at least dress well for the special occasion. No more linen workgowns or homespun shawls, she thought, pulling on a low-cut gown of sage-green silk.

Mrs. McDewey helped her on with tight-fitting gloves and fluffed the silky curls of her shoulder-length hair. Coralee dabbed the essence of lily-of-the-valley on the hollow of Sundra's throat.

"Not too much," cautioned Sundra, a mischievous glint in her sparkling green eyes.

"Methinks ye protest too much," replied Mrs. McDewey. "Hee hee! 'Tis His Grace's fav'rit, and well ye knows it!"

To Sundra's surprise and delight, the duke presented himself and escorted her down the stairs, stopping in the shadows to steal a kiss before guiding her into the grand dining room aglow from the candlelit chandelier. As he held her chair, his eyes looked possessively into hers.

"I'm in a ravenous mood, m'lady," Gardner whispered intimately.

Evans marched ever so gracefully carrying silver trays laden with fragrant delicacies and crystal carafes. Wine was poured, and the duke rose, holding his glass high in the air as he glanced around the stately table until his eyes came to rest on his beautiful wife.

"*Le premier feu*—the first flame—" announced Gardner, raising the glass to his lips as he drank a toast to Sundra.

Modestly Sundra lowered her eyes. It was odd that Charles should feel the need to keep staring at her, she thought, until she noticed what was on her plate. *Quenelles de brochet!* An uncommon recipe consisting of fish dumplings served with a brandy clam sauce; Miriam's favorite dish! Had Charles anticipated a reaction from her? Did he know she was sending money to her cousin behind the duke's back?

"I was hoping you'd like it, Sundra," admitted Charles. " 'Tis my favorite meal."

"Oh?" Alice remarked rather crisply, choosing to ignore the fact that Sundra had pushed away an untouched plate. Ungrateful little chit, she thought. So! The food we eat isn't quite good enough for you either? Hmmp!

Leaving the men to enjoy their cigars and brandy after dinner, the ladies settled into the gilded drawing room resplendent with red brocade furniture and velvet trappings. Alice waited until Sundra was seated and then chose a chair for herself in the opposite corner.

Alice didn't speak, and Sundra wasn't sure how to engage her in conversation.

"Did you know that thousands of birds migrate to Point Pelee in the spring and autumn?" asked Sundra. "I've a journal written by Father Dollier when he had camped there years ago. Would you like me to read it to you?"

"No thank you," replied Alice coolly, pointing her nose up in the air.

Sundra took a deep breath. "No matter, I suppose you'd rather see it firsthand . . . when you're up to it, that is," she added thoughtfully. "It would be a splendid outing."

"Lady Miriam was kind enough to warn me about the foulness of the swamps. Would you wish me to keep company with snakes and mosquitoes?" sneered Alice.

Sundra was shocked. "But the woods are beautiful . . ." she started to say, but let it go at that. She'd never win Alice's friendship by arguing with her.

The boxed present of transparent soap was on the table where Maggie had said it would be waiting. It was now or never, thought Sundra as she handed the gift to Alice.

"'Tis nothing fancy, but it was made especially for you," Sundra said modestly.

Trying not to reveal her fascination, Alice accepted the box and opened it. She instantly uttered a bloodcurdling cry which could be heard throughout the manor, dropping the soap as if it were a hot coal.

"You vicious tart!" hissed Alice, backing up toward the door. "You've just proved how much you hate me!"

Alice ran crying in hysterics as Gardner and Charles came racing into the room. Understandably, Charles did a complete turnabout and went chasing after his wife. Gardner stood with his boots planted firmly apart, scooping up the soapbox in hand.

"I don't know what I could have done to upset her," Sundra said in distress, hastening across the room.

"Suppose you had better start explaining the meaning of this," he demanded acidly, tilting the box for her to see.

Nestled inside the box was a slab of transparent soap all right, but embedded in the center was a tiny dead mouse—its head and tail partially protruding from the waxen bar.

The next day the servants were lined up in the hall while Charles interrogated them individually.

"I can find no fault with the lot of them," Charles later concluded in the duke's presence.

"My staff are loyal to this family, Charles. I trust their honesty."

"Really! Such raffish behavior is a dire insult," scoffed Charles, his face registering a look of indignation as he glanced first at Gardner, then changing his expression to one of pity when his eyes roved over Sundra's trembling body. "Would you believe the servants innocent rather than your wife? Hmph! Then again, if you wouldn't have allowed her to romp with scullions, Alice wouldn't have just cause to blame her!"

"Damn you, I'd call you out if it weren't for Alice," Gardner answered angrily. "And where do you think *you're* going," he asked harshly, suddenly gripping Sundra's tender arm with his hard, biting fingers as she tried to make an exit.

Sundra faced Gardner, trying to regain her composure, her pupils dilated in anger at his skeptical behavior.

"Leave us, Charles," the duke commanded in a harsh tone of voice, ignoring the slamming of the door. Sundra attempted to escape from his arms as he dragged her kicking across the room.

"How dare you think that I could have placed that horrible creature in your sister's soap," gasped Sundra, leaning on the desk for support when Gardner released her none too gently. "I swear to you I'm innocent!"

"Very well, madam," Gardner replied curtly. "I will give you the benefit of the doubt . . . but this," he sneered in contempt, holding up a batch of partially burned papers, "cannot be ignored or denied!"

The duke flung them away in disgust. Half of the pages crumbled to pieces atop the desk and floor, while the other fragments went rippling in the air as it scattered in front of Sundra's horrified face.

With tears blurring her vision, Sundra already knew the pages were from a ledger that had taken weeks for her to complete. Why would anyone want to destroy the hard-earned fruits of her labor, she wondered.

"Why?" repeated Gardner, turning his back on Sundra, silence wedged between them. "Oh, I'll tell you why, madam! One of my banks in London was kind enough to send me a duplicate ledger, requested by my sister because I recently made her a major stockholder in the lumber company. The bank records show that I am fifty thousand pounds overdrawn. Whereas the book you so diligently worked on to complete shows a substantial profit! Clearly you can see the implications, my dear," Gardner said grimly, eying her carefully as he selected a thin cigar from a silver box. He lit it and exhaled the smoke which hid the expression on his face. "How fortunate for me that you failed to completely destroy the evidence—to find you out now, before you included my heart among your damnable accomplishments!"

Sundra raised her hand to strike out at him, only to feel a wrench of pain when Gardner restrained her with a savagely tight grip.

"You're an arrogant fool," cried Sundra, her body trembling, hot tears quelling the fire in her eyes. It was useless to argue with him, she realized. Gardner believed only what he wanted to believe and nothing she could say or do would ever change matters. She had no proof to clear her name and if she did, it was apparently too late. Gardner didn't love her any more than he could trust her. Choosing to save what little pride she had left, she decided to make the first move to end this heartbreaking madness between them.

"Considering that you haven't strung a noose tightly around my neck, I can assumed that I am free to pack my belongings," Sundra pouted, chewing nervously on her lower lip. "I only ask that you arrange passage on the next ship bound for England—and I promise you, Gardner Foxworthy, that on the day I've raised enough money to pay you back for someone else's felony, I shall thank the devil to be freed from you once and for all!"

"How could you do this to me," Gardner beseeched her, pulling her roughly against him. "I would have laid the world at your feet, had you but asked."

"Oh would you now!" replied Sundra curtly. "Precious little was all that you ever promised me," she said, staring boldly to match his fierce gaze. "And you, sir, have the gall to act the injured party! As if I'd lift a finger to swipe your blasted money," she spat. "I was poor when we met. I was poor when we wed. I was poor when you commandeered my dowry and, by all that is holy, I'll be happy to remain poor when I walk out of your life!"

"I should throttle you within an inch of your life and deliver you to Tyburn Prison myself! However, I'll not play the fool twice, madam, for I shall never let you out of my sight!" bellowed Gardner, feeling angrier than he'd ever felt before in his life. He was totally beyond reason. "You lost your precious freedom when you became my wife. You belong to me, forever, and you shall do as I command. From now on your purpose is to serve and please me," he drawled, a hardened smile playing about his lips. "As a Foxworthy, your actions must be beyond reproach. You will dress befitting your station, and I warn you, I will not tolerate you flitting round the estate looking like a Gin Lane ragamuffin. In turn, I will treat you with all due respect and expect the same from you while we are in the presence of others. And if I so desire, you will prove your worth to me . . . in bed," Gardner drawled confidently, keenly aware of the changes taking place, feeling Sundra's tense body growing rigid with fear.

"Y-you'd take me a-against my wishes?" Sundra asked in a shrill voice, aware of the heat generating between their bodies. "Curse you! The devil's burned your ruthless heart to bare ashes!"

"More wishes, m'lady? Make one move to escape me and all you'll have left in this world will be wishes—wildwoods and wishes to be exact," he added. "Take heed, Sundra, that the fire in your eyes and heart doesn't turn your wildwoods and wishes into cold ashes as well."

CHAPTER 9

This is breakfast? Sundra pondered in silence, struggling with the rumpled sheet as she stared in amazement at the tray balanced on her lap.

Lake Erie perch, poached and simmering in a white sauce and thick slices of bacon were nestled around a fluffy mound of mushroom omelet. Butter drop biscuits spread with wild blueberry jam and a side dish of apple dumpling lay next to a steaming hot cup of India tea.

"I can't possibly eat all of this," declared Sundra.

"No? Then I'll not step a fut oot the door until ye does," said Mrs. McDewey matter-of-factly, yanking open the curtains only to find raindrops licking the window panes. Next she waddled over to the armoire and rejected a fine glazed cotton dress for a mauve crepe gown fashioned with a narrow skirt and short bodice. "Ye'll wear this fer aft'noon tea, m'lady."

Sundra grimaced. Having played hostess all week long for afternoon tea was beginning to grate on her nerves. Why should she wear something so special? Gardner and Dr. Todd hadn't the slightest notion of what she had worn before today. All they were interested in, Sundra felt certain, was to scrutinize her manners and ability to act the proper tea-pourer!

"If I'm to be put through my paces, I may as well do it in style," she remarked, a glum expression shadowing her face.

Sundra finally made her appearance downstairs just as Gardner was seeing Captain Wickham to the door. Dr. Todd dashed inside, shaking the rain off his greatcoat while the butler, unperturbed, casually bided his time to help the flustered physician with his wrapper.

As introductions were being made, Sundra took a shy step

backward, standing clear of the hearty back slaps and vigorous handshaking. To her dismay, the captain didn't waste any time taking advantage of standing alone with her—which did not escape her husband's attention. Sundra would have made a hasty retreat had it not been for the frown Gardner cast her way. Defiantly, she firmly stood her ground.

Damn it, thought Gardner, wishing that Wickham had left hours ago. Now, it seemed, he had no other choice but to extend his hospitality to the captain who was ogling his wife. Within a matter of seconds Gardner stood close to Sundra, his eyes demanding the captain's attention.

"Perhaps you'd care to stay and join us for tea?" requested the duke. " 'Tis my wife's favorite part of the day, isn't that so, m'lady?" he laughed, pressuring her arm with his fingers.

"Y-yes!" she added quickly, stifling the heated retort which her husband deserved. "By all means, Captain Wickham, you must stay and be our guest."

"Jonathan," corrected the captain, grinning his acceptance.

Sundra found it rather amusing to have Jonathan's undivided attention, as long as Gardner was aware of it. She had to force herself to act the complaisant wife. Gardner was making it impossible for her to enjoy the occasion. His possessive eyes followed her everywhere. When they were seated together, the pressure of his thigh against hers was enough to unnerve her. Slowly she was losing her haughty composure and, what was worse, Gardner knew it.

"Trentbay," Jonathan spoke abruptly, "you're a devilish rogue for what you've done to Lady Sundra!"

Gardner's muscles grew taut as he leaned menacingly forward, the scowl on his face causing the chatter in the room to cease.

Jonathan plucked another scone from the Spode plate, mindless of the tense situation. Only when his chubby fingers pushed the last bite into his mouth, did he continue. "You've taken away the last hope us bachelors ever had of finding the perfect wife. 'Tis just like you to have found such a treasure and marry her before any of us had the chance to compete for her lovely hand."

Gardner threw back his head, booming with laugher. "Lud, Wickham! You? Compete?" The duke scoffed at the notion and laid a cosseting arm around Sundra's shoulder.

"Sir James claims that you, sir, are an obsessive brute and I'm thoroughly inclined to believe him," jested the red-faced captain. "Alas, you've deeply injured what's left of my common pride, Trentbay, which leaves me no other recourse than to beg your charming wife to grant me a dance on Sunday."

"Sunday?" Sundra pondered out loud, thoroughly bewildered.

"Ah yes, General Engmann's rout," said Dr. Todd. "Indeed, Lady Sundra, if I weren't so decrepit, I'd show this young woebegone pup how not to tread on such delicate feet such as yours. Consider yourself fortunate to have such a fine gentleman for a husband who'll, no doubt, rescue you from the tramplings of your many admirers."

"What say you, Trentbay? Do I and Sir James have your permission to sign your wife's dance card?" asked Jonathan.

While Gardner was acting thoroughly amused, Sundra was seething with silent anger. The duke had never mentioned they were going to attend a party and she was certain he would have waited until the eleventh hour to tell her. How dare he think he could put her on public display at such short notice? Besides, she didn't want to face Miriam, who was making another demand for money already sent.

"Gentlemen, you flatter me no end." Sundra spoke softly, rising to stand by the mantel. "However, it wouldn't be possible to leave my sister-in-law unattended while she's recuperating in our home. I would be honored to save you a dance, Jonathan, perhaps another time."

"On the contrary, madam," argued Gardner. "Dr. Todd will agree that Alice can survive on McDewey's ministerings while we're away for a few nights. My sister would be the first to agree that you should leave Tamarack," he said, watching

Sundra's face flush in embarrassment, and added: "in order for you to attend a rout. Besides, we wouldn't dream of offending the general's wife now, would we? You know Lucinda's temper, gentlemen. Can you imagine what she'd do if I didn't take Sundra along—to pass inspection, you might say?"

While Jonathan and Dr. Todd made jovial comments about Lucinda's infamous tongue-lashings, Gardner confronted Sundra, lowering his voice as he leaned closer to her. "You've no choice, my dear. We're going and that is my final say."

"But . . . I can't," pleaded Sundra.

"You can't, or you won't!" demanded Gardner, his whisper sounding harsh to her ears.

"Neither, I mean . . . oh what's the use," she stammered. "I don't know how to dance, Your Grace! Perhaps now you can understand why I am so reluctant to go."

"Then you must be very elated with my final decision," Gardner replied coolly. "Captain Wickham and James Moore, no doubt, will only be too happy to assist you!"

On Friday Sundra found herself watching Coralee and Mrs. McDewey packing her trunk. In an hour she and Gardner would board the sleek *Windancer* anchored alongside the *Northwind*, and sail to Fort Amherstburg for the weekend. Gardner planned to meet with the officers in charge of the Royal Canadian Volunteers, and she would be left at the mercy of the infamous Lucinda—and Miriam.

"I know wot'll take that frown oft yer face," said Mrs. McDewey, directing a motherly smile at Sundra. "I've been able to sit doon and have a good chat with Lady Alice while her husband was oot back helpin' His Grace. She's agreed to forget aboot the past and wants to see ye before ye sail."

Mrs. McDewey's nod was all the encouragement Sundra needed to dash out of her room, sprinting up the corridor to her sister-in-law's bedchamber until she was almost out of breath. She could feel the tremor inside her heaving chest as she entered. Suddenly the bittersweet memories of sharing this very room, and the canopy bed, with Gardner sent her blood racing, weakening her lithe body until she wanted to cry out the injustice of a hollow marriage. Would Gardner ever call out to her in the night again—to speak her name with sincere desire on his lips?

"Sundra! Can't you hear me? I want to know if Charles is anywhere in the hallway?" asked Alice anxiously. "I thought I heard his voice."

"I'm sorry, my thoughts were . . . uh, no, Charles isn't there. He's still down by the south gate with Gardner."

"Then close the door and sit here," said Alice, motioning for Sundra to take the nearest chair. "Do hurry," she ordered impatiently.

"I know my brother does not like to be kept waiting, so I'll not mince words with you, Sundra," declared Alice. "I've been living in agony ever since I . . . lost my child, and I admit that the shocking circumstances surrounding my brother's hasty marriage has only complicated my tormented thoughts. I can only say that McDewey's helped me see things more clearly and I trust her judgment. That is why I must apologize for having blamed you for putting that rodent in my soap."

"Oh, Alice, you don't know how much I wanted you to accept me into the family," Sundra replied sincerely.

"I said I was sorry, but there are questions pertaining to your marriage which still need to be answered, matters which even McDewey could not explain."

"There are?" Sundra exclaimed, puzzled. "Surely Gardner has taken you into his confidence."

"I can see for myself! This whole arrangement leaves me in distress! Surely you cannot be happy living this way. Why do you punish yourself and not leave here to make a better life for yourself elsewhere?"

"I tried to go away after I realized my mistake, but Gardner wouldn't allow me to return to England," cried Sundra.

"Pah! You didn't try hard enough, girl," scolded Alice. "My brother is a very proud man. Do you realize he's only keeping you here because of his guilty conscience? His honorable pride has been injured and he's too stubborn to admit he's made a mistake in obligations."

"Then what you're saying is that I should try to leave him?" Sundra spoke sullenly.

"I'm only thinking what's best for the two of you," explained Alice. "If it was love you were after, you should know by now that Gardner is incapable of fulfilling your needs. If there be a lady in Gardner's future, then let him be free to choose his own devilish fate."

Sundra had never thought Gardner might have been too arrogant to admit he wanted his freedom as much as she did. It was only natural for him to provide for her after he had spent her dowry. Another woman in his life? Did Alice know something but fear to broach such a delicate subject?

"I didn't mean to confuse you, Sundra. You had best go off to your weekend social. Just think about what I've said and perhaps by the time you return, you'll have reached a decision. I may be able to help you, financially of course."

"I'll give the matter a great deal of thought," promised Sundra, brushing back her tumbled curls.

"One more thing! Your wedding ring had belonged to my mother. Please, see that nothing happens to it?" pleaded Alice. "I couldn't bear to have it lost again."

Sundra understood all too clearly how much the gold ring meant to Alice. Did it matter if she gave it back to her now or later? Probably not, thought Sundra. Swiftly, she handed the ring to Alice and left the room before her tears would be noticed.

Coralee was the first person to spy the ring's absence on Sundra's finger. "Always givin'. . . never takin'," she scolded.

"You're beginning to sound like Mrs. McDewey. Hush now, do you want the duke to hear about this? I can just imagine what he'd have to say, and I'm in no mood to throw myself at his feet with an explanation he'll not listen to!"

"Indeed," came a menacing voice, echoing from the hall.

Instinctively Sundra's left hand shot behind her back. The instant she realized the duke's eyes had been fixed on her all along, she knew she had made a fatal mistake. There was no denying she had put him in a very dangerous mood.

"Alice was afraid I'd lose it and I didn't want her to worry all the while we were gone," confessed Sundra.

"What, your hand?" sneered Gardner, the muscles in his cheek twitching in maddening spasms.

"No this," stammered Sundra, holding out her unadorned hand, allowing her actions to speak louder than words.

In a much controlled voice, Gardner ordered Sundra to wait for him downstairs while he stomped down the hall toward his sister's bedchamber.

What was said or done Sundra would never know, but she had plenty of time to think about it in the solitude of her cabin, the pressure of Gardner's hand when he had replaced the golden ring on her finger served as a reminder of their altercations.

The tip of Point Pelee was coming into view on the starboard side as Sundra was peering out the diamond-paned windows. She had been awed by many fascinating tales about the beautiful peninsula, and it seemed she couldn't let the strange piece of land pass by without giving it a better glimpse; the mystique of the wilderness was that overwhelming to her.

Aware the duke was preoccupied with the *Windancer*'s crew, yet close at hand, she evasively found her way on deck and took a partially concealed seat atop the signal-flag locker.

Pictured before her was a mixture of hardwoods, a wetland forest, and a labyrinth of marshland and dunes. The miles of white, sandy beaches running parallel, converging into a barren point, had captured her attention. Sundra made a promise to herself that she would one day stand on the very tip—where the meeting waters persisted to churn in wild aggression, where sea gulls hovered and flapped cadence in the wind, the shrill of their cry lending an aura of eerie excitement.

The *Windancer* docked at Fort Amherstburg by six o'clock that evening. During a silent dinner in the great-cabin, Sundra was wondering how to approach her husband about what time they would be going ashore. Gardner made it quite clear he was not in the mood for her company, let alone conversation.

Finally, as the duke was preparing to leave the table, he broke the tension in the room. "So"—his lip curled slightly—"you've managed to keep out of harm's way long enough to make amends for your folly this morning. I do hope this is a sign of good behavior?"

"Then you'll be taking me ashore before it grows dark?" asked Sundra, ignoring the duke's insolent manner.

"Tomorrow will be soon enough to turn you loose upon the countryside," he sighed, noticing the disappointed frown on her face, which she tried to hide. "I've important matters which need my immediate attention. If it will make you feel any better, I confess I'm not looking forward to going into Amherstburg any more than you're satisfied staying on board."

"I'll be perfectly fine where I'm at," spoke Sundra, much too quickly. Why did she always have to agree with him?!

As Gardner walked to the Whiskey-Jay Tavern he thought about Sundra's submissive behavior. It wasn't like her not to put up a battle, especially when he knew he had one coming. Had she somehow discovered that his heart was still attached to her no matter how ruthless a fool he acted trying to deny it?

Gardner couldn't figure out Alice's behavior of late either. Whatever possessed that woman to badger Sundra out of her own wedding ring! Was Charles ignorant of Alice's sudden desire for material gain? It seemed strange Alice took comfort in owning stocks, although Gardner had to admit the effect of growing richer did change his sister's condition for the better. He'd do anything to help her, yet somehow he wasn't satisfied by the way things were turning out.

"Still sporting a brooding temper, eh, Trentbay?" James slapped Gardner on the back as he sat down at their private table.

"To hell with me, then," said Gardner, his voice cracking with a hearty laugh. "You bloody ox! It's about time you showed your ugly face around here again. How have you been?"

"Worse for wear, judging by your looks," replied James. "Not to mention a broken arse for helping you with your, uh, certain problem. Do you see that sniveling bugger over there?" he asked, pointing a discreet finger at Fishbait Gilly. "He's proved to be our most valuable source of information. A little addled in appearance perhaps, but the little bastard speaks and acts as though he's just down from Oxford!"

In a lowered voice, James told Gardner what little news he had scrounged up. The lumber company's ledgers had been tampered with for quite some time. Two people were suspected of filling their pockets. Even General Engmann couldn't pay his officers because the payroll had been "misplaced." Gilly swore the two incidents were related.

"Damn!" Gardner cursed, his face darkening with a scowl. "Is that all you could get out of him?"

James threw up his hands as a gesture of wonderment. "Who's to say? His lady friend certainly was convinced that the spirits would take care of the culprits."

"I thought you said you were alone," retorted Gardner. "So help me, James, if I've sent a boy to do a man's work . . ."

"How the hell were we to know the woman was cowering behind some bushes! Besides, her spirit tale was really quite interesting."

"Oh, do tell," sneered the duke.

"Now hear me out," demanded James, freshening their port. "Although the wench wouldn't give names, she claims to have worked for one individual who beat her when she asked for her hard-earned wages. So she stole a lock of that person's hair, along with a love locket she'd discovered in her employer's secret cache, and trotted off to seek her revenge. She sealed the braids inside a tree. When the spirits are ready, they will serve justice to the land when the sap in the tree rises above the spot where the hair is hidden. The braids symbolize a trapped victim, and the sap, rising water. Hence, the two evildoers' fate will be death by drowning."

"And since you're an educated man, you believed her," scoffed Gardner. "Honestly, James, I could fare better listening to Lucinda's bawdy adventures!"

James acted as though his nose had been pulled out of joint, an antic which never failed to put him back on even terms with Gardner. "Actually, you'll be glad to be attending Lucinda's rout. Lady Miriam is staying with the Engmanns, and I'd wager some light will be shed on your, er, other problem if you were to ask the right questions."

"I don't know if I should thank you or knock off your busybody head! You trust Sundra that much, do you?"

James flashed him a brazen smile. "Just as much as you do, only I'm not afraid to admit it."

"Then it's none of your damned business when I have my questions answered," Gardner remarked complacently, hellbent to meet with Miriam before the hour grew late.

The sun was beginning to rise when Gardner came back aboard the *Windancer*. His meeting with Lucinda's guest had been brief but very enlightening, so much to his satisfaction that he didn't even mind the general's drawing him into an all-night discussion of Indian affairs.

Sundra was dressed and patiently waiting for Gardner to join her for breakfast. She knew he had just returned from Amherstburg yet did not make a fuss over his whereabouts. She'd been frightened during the night but worried about his safety rather than her own—and what was her thanks? Nothing but two bloodshot eyes commanding her to scrape his burnt toast!

She knew better than to let the sparks fly in anger, vowing Gardner would not have the satisfaction of predicting her actions anymore. Yesterday, Gardner had told her: "I know you like a book!" Nothing could have irked her more.

"Your business went well, I hope?" said Sundra demurely.

"Much," mumbled Gardner, attacking the beefsteak with his fork and knife.

"I can imagine," she replied politely, passing the salt cellar across the table.

Sundra felt his eyes upon her while she stirred sugar in her tea, returning his gaze with a dazzling smile.

"Confound it, Sundra! I can stand no more of this self-posses-sion of yours. What mischief-making are you up to now?"

"Why nothing, Your Grace," came her innocent reply. "I've merely turned into the docile wife you've wanted me to be. Honestly, I couldn't be more pleased that we are not at odds."

"For the time being, you mean," he growled, watching her fold her napkin and walk serenely toward the door.

"I think you should have some privacy to dress before we go ashore," she spoke calmly. "Which reminds me! May I please have a gown made when we return to Tamarack?"

"If you wish," he replied.

"Good!" conceded Sundra, quickly bending over as she plucked a long strand of blond hair from Gardner's coat, daring to dangle it high in the air. "Then I should like the gown to match the color of this!" She let go, and the strand of hair fell onto Gardner's plate. Sundra made a swift exit without slam-ming the door too hard, vowing she'd rather choke first than to ever wear such a gown!

No sooner had Sundra and Gardner alighted from the car-riage than the general and his wife descended upon them, sweeping the couple into the house as greetings were made dur-ing the shuffle of baggage.

Lucinda's raucous laughter filled the foyer, as she threw her arms around Gardner for the second time. "Just like old times!" she was delighted to say, devilishly pleased to see the faint trace of a blush on Gardner's face. Reaching out, she pulled Sundra into their tight circle. "Why, you're such a little thing!" she mocked kindly. "You sure as 'ell got your hands full managing this brute, eh?" she claimed.

"Lucinda, please! You're embarrassing the poor girl," scolded the general.

"Nonsense, George! Sundra and I are going to get along just fine, and the sooner she knows I don't mince words, the better off we'll be. Besides, the duke here probably stuffed cotton in her ears to spite me!" Lucinda laughed merrily.

"I wouldn't dream of blocking out your lovely voice," bantered Gardner, "but now that you've mentioned it, perhaps George and I will be needing some in due time."

"Silly goose," Lucinda sniffed out loud. "I couldn't care a fig what you do!"

As much as the general and the duke pretended they wanted to join the ladies in the parlor, excuses were made so the men could finish discussing Indian Territorial rights in private.

Sundra found the atmosphere refreshing—despite Lucinda's long mane of blond hair—and they exchanged similar views on a variety of subjects, including husbands, which sealed their bond of friendship.

"I like you," Lucinda admitted candidly. "You're not at all stuffy even though you're a duchess. Oh, I can't wait to show you off to my guests! Half of them are probably coming to my rout just as an excuse to catch a glimpse of the new Duchess Trentbay, but," she exclaimed, throwing up her hands, "who cares! The Royal Canadian Volunteers are coming and we'll have a jolly good time with that bunch."

"I'm looking forward to it," Sundra said in earnest, although she wished there would be more ladies in attendance. "I've recently met Jonathan Wickham, and I'm anxious to see James Moore again too. He sailed with us on the *Northwind*."

"Ah, that Jamie's a dear! In fact, you just missed seeing him," replied Lucinda. "'Course I was ready to throw his arse out anyhow . . . kept eating chunks out of the queen's cake reserved for the party! Which reminds me, I'd better stick my nose in the kitchen already."

"Is there anything I can do for you?" offered Sundra.

"Not a thing, dearie," chortled Lucinda. "I'll have cook prepare us some sassafras tea."

"How very nice of you," replied Sundra. "I'd enjoy a cup right now." She smiled as Lucinda turned and paused in the doorway.

"You know, your cousin and me were sort of friends years ago when St. James's Street amused us. In fact, I'll go and tell her to keep you company while I check on things."

Sundra didn't relish the idea of coming face to face with Miriam—not yet, especially since she hadn't put her troubled thoughts in order.

"Didn't your father ever teach you that even ladies of Quality must pay the piper?" cackled a feminine voice. "You're late with another payment, as usual!"

"Miriam!" breathed Sundra. "But I've already given you all of the household purse! I don't dare ask Gardner for more."

"Oh, he's suspicious of you, all right," retorted Miriam.

Sundra bit her lower lip, taking a deep breath as she steadied herself against the love seat.

"I know everything," declared Miriam smugly, "including your loveless marriage, at least from the duke's point of view. Tell me, how does it feel to love a man who thinks so very little of you," she asked slyly, "and he being a murderer at that!"

"I won't stand here and listen to any more of your lies," exclaimed Sundra, stamping her foot.

"Oh? I dare you to make inquiries about the ring you're wearing. Gardner took it from Adrian Shaw, who was shot dead not ten paces away from him while witnesses looked on, including James Moore!"

"Just what are you getting at?" demanded Sundra, wishing Lucinda would walk in to put an end to this discussion.

"I cannot live on the pittance you've given me," Miriam replied bluntly, and hinted about the possibility of blackmailing Gardner in return for her silence about Shaw's death. "But then, if anything were to happen to His Grace, the payments would stop . . . and you, my dear, would inherit nothing! His sister would, and I'm very much aware that nothing could please her more than to throw you out on your ear," snickered Miriam. "You don't belong here, Sunny. So why don't you return to the vicarage and leave me to settle the matter with Gardner? What I do to get my hands on his money after you've gone is none of your concern, but I do promise to take good care of him."

Sundra flew into a rage. No matter what Gardner thought of her, she would warn him by exposing Miriam's greedy quest.

Under no circumstances was she going to allow her cousin to ruin *his* life as she'd tried to do with hers.

"Why are you hesitating?" hissed Miriam. "You little fool! I'll be saving Gardner's life, if I can get close to him. If not, he's a dead man for certain. Listen here, young lady, I can't take the chance that someone will get rid of the duke and keep the wealthy estate for himself!"

"You sound as though you already know someone is plotting against Gardner, don't you?" asked Sundra frantically.

"Charles Hewett!" came the accusing answer. "I've known him since his bachelor days and I'm well aware of the trouble he can cause. Either I live with Gardner as his new duchess, or I'll continue to conspire with Charles, who's going to make sure he inherits the Foxworthy empire very soon. It matters not which man warms my bed, as long as I'm wealthy. Accept my alternative, Sunny," urged Miriam, "or you'll be putting your husband's life at stake."

Footsteps in the hallway forced Miriam into action. She rushed over to Sundra and, pulling out a pistol from her pocket, pointed it at her trembling cousin.

"I'm desperate, damn you!" Miriam cursed hoarsely. "If you ever repeat what's just been discussed between us, I swear I'll put a bullet in Gardner's head and think naught of what I've done to him! 'Tis your choice . . . leave him, or love him—dead in his grave!"

"Ah, there you are, ladies," beckoned Lucinda, strutting into the parlor, while Miriam quickly hid the gun behind her back.

"Oh, Lucie," Sundra hurriedly whispered, "I don't want to be rude, but I've developed a terrible headache and I think it would be best if I took a nap before dinner."

"It was a pleasure to be with you again, Cousin," Miriam called out sweetly. "We'll continue our little chat soon, eh?"

As Gardner was holding open the study door while the footman brought in another bottle of port, he caught a glimpse of Sundra running up the staircase. Confound that girl, he thought in dismay. Why did she have to run with her skirt hiked up, exposing her slender ankles for the servants to gawk at!

"As I was saying, Trentbay," snorted George. "We're caught in a devilish position. Another band of Shawnee were uprooted from the Ohio Valley and I promised to help them relocate north of here. Only problem is, with the flow of Americans into our community, I fear tensions will arise over who will inhabit the prime areas. I dare to say John Simcoe may be getting carried away by his eagerness to see Upper Canada populated. His generous land grants to convert the Americans can only last so long before we run out of space."

"You know my sympathies lie with both parties, George," replied Gardner. "A man should be free to settle wherever he wishes, as long as others don't suffer. But . . . there'll always be battles like Fallen Timbers, and my personal opinion is not enough to change matters until this frontier settles down. I'm surprised the Indians remained down in the valley this long. The tribes ceded their land three years ago."

"'Tis a good thing Dorchester isn't here to hear you say that," scoffed the general. "After the Indian buffer state collapsed, he still fears the repercussions will eventually affect our western posts, whether it be from the Indians or the United States."

Drinking freely, the two men discussed their points of view, the light of day waning. York was the topic of conversation when Lucinda intruded upon their privacy.

"Dammit, George!" she said irately, hands on her hips as she squarely faced her flushed husband. "You've been shut up in this room long enough! Our guests are preparing for dinner and I don't want you to be late just because you're talking about some village noted for its mud!"

The duke, amused by the general's flustered state, stood silently in the background. Nothing George could say or do would budge Lucinda from the study!

"You amaze me, Lucie," commented Gardner, flashing her a wicked smile. "Since when have you cared if George or I dined on time?"

"Since George let me have my first Canadian party tomorrow, that's why, ducky! I'm making sure everyone in these backwoods has a roaring good time . . . and don't tell me you don't miss tearing up the town like we used to do in London. Ain't that so, George? George!"

"Trentbay's a married man now, Lucie," replied the general, wiping his brow. "Perhaps it is by his good choice that he prefers not to go merrymaking all over the territory with Sundra the way you want me to do with you. A man's got to take time to settle down, you know."

"And I should be so lucky not to have a headache from being stuck in the mud either!" retorted Lucinda. " 'Tis a wonder that Sundra didn't get a migraine long before today."

The upstairs was a quiet haven, yet Sundra was not successful at putting her mind at ease. For an hour she had been in tears and had to put a cold cloth over her red and swollen eyes.

How many times must I be hurt before I realize my romantic notions mean nothing but trouble, thought Sundra. Miriam had no right to threaten Gardner's life if she didn't leave him. She had no choice in the matter now. If she wished to try and make her marriage work, Gardner wouldn't live long enough to know how much his wife truly loved him.

Love? Suddenly it dawned on Sundra what had been plaguing her thoughts all along. "I love him," she said, amazed she could finally admit the truth about the man who had denied her everything except heartache. And still, she wanted Gardner more than anything else in this world.

How could she slip away from Gardner's life without arousing his suspicion? Having acted the complaisant wife these past few days wasn't going to make her bid for freedom any easier. If anyone was going to get rid of her, it would have to be the duke himself! She had to make him realize it was a mistake for him to keep her in wedlock when he didn't even love her. "By the time I'm finished with him, he'll be glad to rid himself of an unwanted wife!" vowed Sundra.

Guests were arriving on foot, horseback, and by the wagonload. The men had donned uniform to proudly proclaim their rank in the regiment. A few locals fidgeted in borrowed suits, while the backwood scouts who detested unbending attire stood comfortably in buckskins. The array of ballgowns ran the gamut from simple calicoes to stunning cremosin creations.

Sundra entered the mirrored ballroom, on her husband's arm, her eyes wide with apprehension yet sparkling in excitement when the music began and the guests started forming a circle for the round dance. The soft kidskin dancing slippers on her feet served as a reminder of her inexperience. Her heart began pounding more rapidly as she watched Captain Wickham heading straight toward her to claim the first dance.

Sundra would have gone to meet Jonathan halfway if the duke hadn't restrained her by the arm. Regardless of her near *faux pas*, she smiled at the captain when he greeted her with an impressionable deep bow.

Gardner raised an eyebrow. "Ah, Wickham! So nice of you to be the first to dance with my wife . . . after me, of course," he remarked casually, sloughing off the man as he smugly led Sundra away on his arm.

Sundra suddenly balked from leaving her spot once the circle of dancers began moving.

"I will lead you with my hand and body movements," directed Gardner. "As for your feet, watch the ladies across the way and copy their steps . . . and smile, for heaven's sake," he urged her, spinning her around when the rhythm of the music caught up to them.

At first Sundra totally relied on Gardner's guidance, then as the circle flowed merrily roundabout, she found her feet moving with a grace of their own.

"It has been a pleasure, madam," commented Gardner, watching Sundra trying to suppress a smile. "Besides, I wouldn't dream of letting anyone else step on my toes the way you did."

"How kind of you to notice," she replied coldly. "Perhaps Jonathan wouldn't mind being my next victim," she said coyly, granting him a delicately shy smile.

"Oh, indeed not, m'lady," chuckled Jonathan, "nor would the other gents, judging by your filled dance card!"

Instead of retreating to the gaming room, Gardner stood in the archway, alarmed to see the bachelors clustered by the edge of the dance floor. Why, they were openly leering at his wife while she danced with an attentive partner, only to be swept away by someone else when the music changed tunes. What's more, Sundra seemed to be enjoying every minute of attention!

Gardner set up a watch post by the silver punch bowl and, as Sundra danced beyond his view, he had to rescue Lucinda when she lost her balance while frolicking on the cloak table.

"Oh, don't look so damned disgusted while I'm in your arms, Gardner," giggled Lucinda, realizing his attention was focused elsewhere. "Lud! You shouldn't have brought Sundra if you didn't want those young bucks twirling her around!"

"Need I remind you that your last rout in London nearly ended in a riot of jealous husbands? Besides, Sundra may be a little too naïve to see where all this frivolity is leading if she doesn't watch her step."

"Jealous husbands, my arse!" retorted Lucinda, deposited on her own two feet. "All Sundra is doing is having fun, which is more than I can say for reformed rakes such as yourself."

Thirty minutes had flown past when Sundra finally made her way back to Gardner's side. Her face was flushed, darkening into a rosy hue of embarrassment when six cups of punch were offered to her simultaneously by the young men who had followed after her. Gardner dispersed them with a menacing scowl.

"You've done yourself proud, madam, for someone who's never danced a step in her life before tonight," Gardner commented sarcastically.

Sundra lifted her nose in the air and choked back her retort in the nick of time. James Moore had approached them and, to Sundra's surprise, Miriam was hanging onto his arm.

"Sorry we're late," said James.

Gardner took Miriam's hand and raised it to his lips.

"And I too, must apologize . . . for leaving you so abruptly last evening," murmured Gardner, watching out of the corner of his eye for Sundra's reaction.

"How gallant you are," cooed Miriam, slightly parting her

painted lips. "Were you so fascinated with Lucinda, Your Grace, that you forgot to ask me for a dance?"

"I would be delighted, madam, but I've already promised the next set to my wife," replied Gardner.

"Please, I'm much too tired to take another step," pleaded Sundra. "By all means dance with Miriam, Gardner."

Sundra continued to smile even as her heart was breaking to watch Gardner contemplating the dance floor with Miriam latched onto his proffered arm. Would Lucinda be claiming him next, she wondered.

"You look as though you could stand a breath of fresh air," offered James, "although I think you would look much happier if Gardner had asked to take you outdoors instead of me."

"Don't be contrite, James," scolded Sundra. "His Grace would never have asked, and I wouldn't have accepted if he did!"

They escaped to the open balcony and found a seat overlooking the twinkling lights in the harbor.

"You're very beautiful tonight, Sundra," said James, gently lifting her chin, "even though you try not to frown. Why don't you tell me what's troubling you? I'd make a very good listener."

"You're very kind, Jamie," answered Sundra, "but I'm perfectly fine! I'm exhausted from all that dancing and I'm glad Miriam showed up because I couldn't have taken another step."

"You don't fool me, m'lady. You're letting Miriam lead Gardner around by the nose! Why?"

"You shouldn't say such a foolish thing," said Sundra, cautiously, holding her breath as the strains of music flowed beyond the french doors.

"Don't," warned James, forcing her to look him straight in the eye. "Are you forgetting I'm the same person you confided to on the *Northwind?* Sundra! I've believed in you from the beginning. If you're in any sort of trouble I want to help you. Come on," he coaxed, pulling her closer to comfort her as a friend. "I've got a broad shoulder for you to cry on."

Sundra had to muster her courage to keep from doing just that. She longed with all her heart for James to help her, but knew better than to possibly endanger his life with a problem she alone must solve.

"Yesterday, I was a young girl with foolish dreams. Whatever I said then means nothing to how I feel now. You would be sadly mistaken, James, to think otherwise," replied Sundra.

"Are you implying you've made amends with Miriam? You'd be making a terrible mistake!"

"She's my family," remarked Sundra quickly, "and I plan on asking her to join us at Tamarack if she'll come. Now, if you don't mind, I would like to go back inside—alone."

At the head of the stairs, Sundra paused uncertainly, gazing over her shoulder to find Miriam staring up at her with a smile of approval on her smug face. From a distance Gardner was crossing the room holding two glasses of champagne and, without a moment's notice, Miriam flew to his unsuspecting side, coyly leading him farther back into the ballroom lest he should spy his wife who deserted the party.

In the early hours of the morning Sundra heard a shuffle in the adjoining room her husband occupied. When the doorknob turned ever so slightly she quickly blew out the candle. She was glad to have locked the door—not so much to keep the duke away, but for herself, afraid she might lose her willpower and rush into his arms and never wish to leave.

After a sleepless night, Sundra was relieved only a few stragglers had found their way downstairs for breakfast. She saw Miriam, who had never risen from bed before noon in years, finishing her tea. With Lucinda as a handy witness, Sundra cordially invited Miriam to visit with her and the duke.

"Oh, how very kind of you to ask," gushed Miriam. "But the truth of the matter is that His Grace has already asked me!"

Thankfully, the *Windancer* made record-breaking time sailing from Amherstburg, around the shrouded Point, to anchor offshore at Tamarack.

Alice and Charles were playing cribbage in the study when

Gardner presented his beguiling guest. Sundra avoided looking at Charles—which her husband secretly noted on his list of her odd actions of late.

The next morning Sundra arranged to take Miriam on a tour of the estate. With Mrs. McDewey's guidance, the trio converged on the third floor of the grand manor, working their way down to the underground tunnel leading to the fieldstone cookhouse.

Kip saddled two horses and waited patiently while Miriam finished inspecting the stables.

"Very good work, my boy," praised Miriam, patting Kip's tufted hair.

Only Sundra noticed Miriam disdainfully wiping off her hand after the boy had bent down to aid Miriam in mounting the horse.

As they rode along the cobbled courtyard, Miriam kept her eyes glued on the west wing and terrace which housed Gardner's study and library. Sundra pointed to the square-roofed turrets on the opposite sides atop the third floor. The gatekeeper raised his clay pipe in greeting as he opened the whitewashed palisade gate. When they reached the south gate, the two women scanned the endless horizon on the edge of Lake Erie. Wilderness flanked the cleared fields where workers tilled the soil in readiness for the tobacco seedlings. Miriam grew weary and did not wish to linger in the hothouses or warming barns to inspect the plants. At a brisk trot, they returned to the estate, where Sundra introduced Miriam to Dr. Todd after a tour of the infirmary.

While Miriam and Alice were enjoying tea, Sundra dashed upstairs to her room. She knew without a doubt she would have to leave soon, judging by the way Miriam was quickly adapting to living in the country.

Sundra tried to remain inconspicuous, giving Miriam a free hand to become involved with the lives around her. Sundra did not come into contact with her servant friends any more than was necessary and discouraged their attempts to draw her into a friendly conversation. She couldn't look straight into anyone's face except Evans's, whose emotionless stare she returned in earnest.

Soon conversations came to a halt whenever Sundra came into a room. After a while the servants didn't bother to stop gossiping, whispering as their eyes followed her out of the area. Only Coralee was brave enough to repeat the tales of the servant's grapevine. The family thought the duke was finally coming to his senses, bringing home such a kind and charming lady as Miriam, especially since the present duchess was becoming an intolerably standoffish person! More stones to shatter Sundra's dreams.

Gardner and Charles were overly attentive to Miriam's slightest whims. Sundra could just about imagine Charles's ulterior motives but didn't know why Gardner went to such great lengths to please Miriam in her presence when he had ignored her at other times.

Sundra knew her plan was working by the end of the week. Even the staff paid no attention to her comings and goings as they had before. If only they knew how disheartened she felt to think her presence in the manor mattered naught to the people she loved. Gardner was not quite the demanding husband, although his eyes openly reprimanded her for staying away.

The men had gone out to inspect the fields and the servants scattered to loaf in hiding. Sundra prepared a steaming milk bath for Miriam to soak in. There were several fashion plates in the library Miriam wanted to look at, and she sent Sundra to fetch them.

The library was quiet, save for the ticking of the clock on the mantelpiece. Of all the rooms in the manor, the master bedchamber aside, Sundra was going to miss this one the most. She had read volumes of history, Latin and such, gingerly turning the pages while fingering the rich leather covers. She took pride in her self-schooling, modest of her many accomplishments.

"Looking for something special?" asked a familiar voice, startling Sundra back to reality.

Turning, Sundra's face was expressionless as she gave her reply to the duke. "I have what Miriam wanted," she said civilly. She gathered her taffeta skirt and prepared to step aside in order to avoid coming into close contact with her husband.

Gardner walked slowly toward her, as if stalking his prey. Sundra could almost feel the barely restrained violence of his body as he halted before her, blocking any path of escape.

"This game of ours has gone on long enough," he sneered. "Damn it! I cannot tolerate the cowardly ninnyhammer you've become!"

"'Tis what you've wished for! Honestly," she sighed heavily, "I can see you'll never be satisfied with anything I do! Indeed, you've much to be desired yourself. Why not admit that you've made a mistake by keeping me against my will and be done with it? I'll not be too expensive for holding my tongue."

"Look at me," Gardner demanded harshly, but Sundra could only stare into space, her mind filled with tormented thoughts about the cruel part she must now play. "When I asked Miriam to join us, I thought she was all the reason I needed to snap you out of your foolish charades. You have wildfire coursing through your veins and I've come to realize the only mistake I've made was thinking I could tame that high spirit of yours. Yet, you have let me browbeat you and treat you shamefully without putting up a fight. I cannot stand it when you act meekly, as though you are begging for more punishment. You've all but placed your wedding ring on Miriam's finger!" he sneered, his lip curling with disgust. "I demand the reason for your insolent behavior!"

There was silence in the room. Sundra dare not breath lest he should become aware of her trembling body. She had built a wall of resistance between them, and it was now or never to make her bid for freedom—however painful it may be.

"I'm surprised you have the audacity to stand there simplemindedly and ask me," she replied tartly. "I thought I made it quite clear what I think about our mockery of a marriage. My dowry was the only reason why I married you, and when I realized I would never get my money's worth living in these godforsaken wildwoods of yours, I played the vixen, the complaisant wife . . . anything . . . just to make your life hell until you release me from our vows," she said, her eyes blazing in anger at her own lies, her breasts heaving from the outburst. "Take the opportunity to give Miriam your attention. She offers you a good excuse to be rid of me. I don't want to obey your commands or fulfill your desires, nor do I want to raise your sniveling little brats while you, sir, play lord of the wilderness! There's no room in my life for you! . . ."

Sundra flinched at the sound of books crashing to the floor, the violence of Gardner's action making her cringe behind a highback chair for protection. Gardner merely kicked it aside with his boot and reached for her, grabbing her shoulders with his muscular hands.

"You dare tell me more lies?" he growled ominously, his eyes smoldering with rage. "No matter how foolishly you try, madam, you cannot play me for the fool! Have you forgotten that it was your innocence which saved me from my anger when I wanted to murder Elliot Spencer for touching you? I've been watching with my own eyes just how much you love living and working at Tamarack . . . and most important of all, you let me make love to you in such a special way that my heart is yours for the taking? By God, Sundra, could you leave me now and say these things you've done, did not matter at all? . . . Tonight I'm going to show you, my dear, how very real our marriage can be, and will be! And in the morning, I dare you to tell me face to face that I mean nothing to you!"

Sundra backed up a step, afraid of what Gardner was implying. He pulled her roughly to him, kissing her with searing, hungry lips. The bold encounter of his kiss took Sundra's breath away. Her head started to whirl as she first felt his tongue, brushing across her lips and then forcing them open.

She wanted to tell him how much she truly loved and needed him, returning his kiss for the last time; for little did he know that if she remained clinging to his lips, it would be like a kiss of death to his future. Deliberately she jerked aside, struggling against her own feelings as much as she did to thwart Gardner's advances. Without a word she ran crying from the room.

Sundra had barely pounced on her bed, her tears falling abandonedly upon the pillow, when Miriam softly padded across the oriental rug to reach her.

"You know what this means, don't you?" asked the uncompassionate Miriam.

"You heard us in the library?"

"Only part of it," Miriam said ruefully, "but enough to know it isn't wise for you to spend another night in this house with him. Your duke, no doubt, will go prowling tonight to satisfy his needs, and it doesn't take love to accomplish the fact, either!"

"And you have me to thank for starving him, is that it? Don't you sing your praises to me, Miriam," warned Sundra. "You know as well as I do that if Gardner had married me for love, I wouldn't need his threats to persuade me to his bed."

With narrowed eyes, Miriam watched Sundra trudge over to a hamper and dig out a meager bundle of clothes, slinging them into a satchel.

"Here's a little something to show you my appreciation," murmured Miriam as she fingered the softness of the blue negligee hanging in the scented armoire before tossing a small pouch of coins at Sundra's feet. "How do you think Gardner will react when he sees me in this," she asked tauntingly, pulling the gown off the hanger.

Sundra had intended to leave the negligee and its memories behind. Suddenly she couldn't bear the thought of Miriam using it to her advantage and, whether it was a change of heart or a futile attempt to strike out against her cousin, she snatched the negligee away from Miriam.

Shamefaced, Sundra rolled it into a ball and added it to her sparse belongings. For once Miriam didn't dispute the matter. Instead, Sundra saw her cousin reach inside the closet and grab up the rest of the silky gowns, holding them possessively against her chest.

Miriam started dancing to a tune known only to herself, swaying and turning merrily round the room until she fell backward onto the bed. Laughter burst from her paint-smeared lips. "Is there anything you want me to whisper in Gardner's ear tonight?" she asked, deliberately thrashing her head from side to side, her body bouncing suggestively on the mattress. She guffawed in delight and snickered out loud when Sundra fled.

While she paused in the pantry to snitch a morsel of food, Sundra carefully plotted her course, knowing she must travel with speed as well as caution, for there were only three hours of daylight left for her journey. Undetected, she escaped from the manor and zigzagged across the meadow until she had safely arrived at the south gate. From there she walked along the shoreline, taking a glimpse at the miles of white fencing behind her every now and again to reassure herself that no one was following her.

Not until she was halfway to Point Pelee did Sundra allow herself to rest for more than five minutes, falling in an exhausted heap on the sandy trail. Overhead the sky was beginning to darken with storm clouds, and she grew worried that her cape would not be enough to keep the rain from soaking her weakened body once the wind kicked up.

She took a few sips from a nearby stream and settled back against an aspen tree while she ate a piece of jerky. During her flight she had not heard a sound in the forest, but now, the calls of the whiskey-jays disturbed her.

"Time stands still for no one, my dear," came a voice from behind the fir tree.

"Charles?" Sundra questioned the invisible intruder.

"Quite right," he replied, remaining hidden by the foliage. "'Tis only fair to warn you that you've left a trail a mile wide behind you. Tsk, tsk, you'd better be more careful!"

"Then you haven't come to stop me?" she queried, her relief suddenly turning into apprehension when Charles stepped into the clearing. He was wearing buckskin breeches and a beaded leather shirt. A quiver of arrows was slung across his shoulder.

"You know, I once rid myself of a thieving charwoman by a mere flogging. But you . . . you are different," he stated nonchalantly, flexing the string on his bow. "I give you my word of honor that I won't budge from this spot until sundown before I go hunting after you."

"Please, Charles," pleaded Sundra, "I don't know what you mean. If you plan on taking me back to Tamarack by force, why not do so now?"

"Take you back?" scoffed Charles. "Dear lady, you don't know how long I've waited for you to run away! Heaven only knows how hard I've prodded Alice to throw you out! Alas, she has a kind heart, a weakness of the spirit, you might say, and she would surely have befriended you if I hadn't convinced her otherwise. She may have offered financial help, but now I'm afraid it's too late to make good your escape, thanks to your cousin Miriam."

"What difference does it make whose word influenced me to leave?" questioned Sundra, a prickling sensation running down her spine as she rose from her spot.

"Knowing Miriam, she probably gave you too much information for your own good about our quest for the Foxworthy empire," Charles replied arrogantly. "Now I'm afraid you'll have to perish because I can't take the risk of you exposing either of us, although I wouldn't be surprised in the least if I had to contend with Miriam as a rival by the time I return home. Now get going," he shouted, raising the bow above his head. "I suggest using your wits, because I can easily follow your trail and hunt you down as I would any other creature in the forest. Keep in mind that my arrows are very sharp and that I will jump at the chance to pierce your heart when the opportunity arises. Giving you a head start merely lends an air of excitement to the chase, don't you agree?"

Impetuously, Sundra seized her satchel, gathered up her skirt, and dashed headlong down the trail while listening to Charles whoop and holler as she scurried for cover.

CHAPTER 10

Recklessly Gardner shoved aside the paper on his desk, his dark mood matching the fury of rain beating against the windows in his study. He poured another brandy, swallowing it with one gulp and then, throwing the glass against the hearth, got up to pace the floor.

The duke was not the type of man who'd use force on any woman, but swore he was at the end of his patience if Sundra did not cooperate with him tonight.

Yet, he couldn't blame her if she didn't. He'd been less than honest with her ever since Lucinda's rout, a chance he had to take, but a move which could very well have cost him his wife.

"A jack of all trades, yet master of none," he murmured, scornful of his own character, ignoring a light rapping on the door. It was opened by Evans, who announced warily:

"Lady Miriam to see you, Your Grace."

Gardner stepped aside as Miriam swept regally into the room, her heady perfume permeating the air.

"Gardner darling! It was very impolite to ignore me during dinner this evening. So, I thought now was as good a time as any to . . . get better acquainted," she uttered coyly.

The duke watched through narrowed eyes as she swayed her hips walking toward him, her white and slender arms reaching out to him. He forced himself to look down into her beseeching eyes, her crimson lips parted, inviting a kiss as she wantonly stroked the back of his neck. Slowly his eyes wandered over her.

Abruptly, Gardner turned away. "I'm a married man," he stated, "and if you think I wanted you here to, shall we say, share my affections, you are sadly mistaken. I apologize for allowing you to believe otherwise."

"Oh I've seen just how happy a marriage you have," she ridiculed sweetly. "Did your wife please you when she didn't even bother to show her face at the table tonight? Hardly!" Miriam scoffed with a laugh. "You were silently livid! Even your sister sat dumbstruck, too afraid to move lest you should suddenly fly into a rage." She moved closer to stand directly in front of him. "A woman can bring out the best in a man. Perhaps all you need is a little encouragement so that I can prove it to you," she whispered suggestively.

"Don't, Miriam!" Gardner said harshly, firmly placing her an arms length away. "I'm well aware of the games you play, although I have no proof to substantiate my claim—yet. The tension in the dining room only made me more aware of the strange goings on here since your arrival, indeed ever since I returned to Canada. Oh yes," he admitted, "Alice was very disturbed, but there's something else bothering her besides worrying why her husband hadn't returned from the hothouses. Was it because he is still out there waiting for you to brave the storm before you have another clandestine meeting? As for my behavior toward my wife, I . . ." he started to say, interrupted by a resounding knock at the door.

"Excuse me, Your Grace," apologized Evans, "but there are some gentlemen here to see you. I tried to tell them you were busy, but Sir James said it was urgent and demanded to see you immediately."

"And not a moment too soon," James said sarcastically, pushing past the butler while his eyes took in Miriam's attire, mistaking the duke's reddened face of anger for the flush of desire. "Gardner, may I present Lieutenant Alexander and Corporals Barlow and Smythe, masters-at-arms, and of course you're already acquainted with Sir Edmund Dillingham over here." He gestured.

There was an ominous murmur in the study as the men exchanged handshakes, gathering in front of the doorway where Miriam almost made good her escape.

"I wouldn't be in such a hurry to get out of here, Lady Miriam," cautioned Sir Edmund. "I can't stand the sight of you, to be sure, but I fear my resentments are mild compared to what Addie Quiggs thinks of you. His Grace's sister and the housekeeper are outside this door trying to calm her down."

"What is the meaning of all this nonsense!" Miriam demanded to know, her voice shrill and piercing.

"Ah, yes," said James, sweeping his arm in her direction. "Perhaps I'd better clarify your presence in Canada to Gardner. Thanks to the diligent efforts of these men, especially Sir Edmund, we have solid evidence that Miriam not only was stealing you blind, but has been extorting money from Lady Sundra!"

"Your Grace, how can you stand there and let this man accuse me of a crime?" screamed Miriam. "Granted, I may have borrowed a few guineas from Sunny . . . but I never touched your ledgers! And I don't need your filthy money either!" She edged closer toward the door, wary of the forboding faces staring at her.

"Lies!" scoffed Sir Edmund, turning to address his brooding audience. "'Twas Lady Miriam's quest for the St. Ives dowry that caused Sundra to flee from her in the first place and, I might add, that forced her into a marriage of convenience—a situation which warrants serious discussion with His Grace if I'm to be satisfied about Sundra's well-being."

"The man's an old foozle! Sundra's merely filled his empty head with lies of her own," retorted Miriam.

"Then perhaps you have an explanation about how you knew my ledgers had been tampered with?" Gardner asked impatiently. "It is not common knowledge."

Startled by the coldness of his voice, Miriam stood uncomfortably for the moment as his dark blue eyes raked her face. Lies spewed forth from her lips, claiming Alice had told her everything. The baroness had the nerve to implicate Charles now that she herself was caught in a precarious position.

James demanded attention by angrily stomping his boot and waved a packet of letters in the air; love letters and detailed instructions Miriam had recently penned to Charles, which he so foolishly did not destroy.

Lieutenant Alexander cleared his throat. "Your Grace, I'm

sorry to say that your brother-in-law is seriously involved in this scandal. With your permission, I should like to question him before I return to Fort Amherstburg with Lady Miriam. Passage has been arranged to transport her back to England where she'll stand trial, and I daresay, there are other people whom she has fleeced that are only too willing to testify against her. I'm not certain what action will be taken against Hewett until I speak with him."

"Idiots!" screamed Miriam, lashing out with her nails as she tried to rush past the men.

Gardner took two giant strides and captured her wrists, handing her none too gently over to the master-at-arms. "Get her out of my sight," he growled, his control snapping in a wave of outraged fury. He snatched the letters from James, issuing orders that Charles be summoned to the room, ignoring the mumbled protests against his violent temper from the barrister. "As for you, Sir Edmund," snarled Gardner, "no one has ever dared to question my actions, least of all from the very man who was more than happy to foist his best friend's daughter on me in the first place."

Sir Edmund felt the blood rushing into his wrinkled face. "Your attitude, Your Grace, is precisely why I question if you are capable of making Sundra's life pleasant," he spoke in disdain, "and I dare to say to you that I was absolutely horrified to hear of the ruthless and barbaric way she's been treated after you failed to deliver her to the vicarage. Rest assured, sir, that I will see to it Sundra has a final say as to her future!"

Gardner threw his arms high in the air, mindless of the screams and kicking as Miriam was being dragged from the room. "James!" bellowed Gardner. "Remove this man before he tempts me to considerably shorten his life . . . and don't you dare to glower at me! You'd like nothing better than to wrench Sundra from life, wouldn't you? You ignorant ox! I will give you an account of my thoughts concerning my marriage when I damn well please! So don't condemn me too soon."

As though the duke needed another calamity to add to the confusion, Alice, Mrs. McDewey and Addie burst into the room, wailing in unison as each raised her voice to outshout the others.

Between sniffles, coughing, and exasperated sighs, the women bemoaned the bad news—Sundra had disappeared! McDewey feared the girl had run away, because her satchel was missing, only to have Addie cluck her tongue, muttering that all those who had neglected her dearest Sunny should have their ears boxed.

" 'Tis shameful behavior is what it is," wailed Addie, sizing up her opponents.

"Oh, Gardner, please forgive me for what I've done," babbled Alice. "I was only thinking of your best interests. You see, I put the notion in Sundra's head to go away. Charles told me that you were too proud to get rid of her yourself, so I thought I was doing you a favor," she confessed in earnest. Judging by the darkened scowl on her brother's face, she felt certain he'd enjoy shaking her by the throat until she dropped.

"My dear Lady Alice," Sir Edmund addressed her with compassion. "Do not be too harsh with yourself. We are all trying to do what's best for each other, and it isn't an easy task, since the duke has yet to share his innermost thoughts. Besides, only Miriam would have the gall to finish whatever you may have tried to uproot Sundra. You do know that your husband is involved in this embezzlement?"

Wiping her eyes, Alice nodded and straightened her shoulders to compose herself. "Not at first," she replied, "but I knew something was tragically wrong with our marriage when I discovered the ledgers he and Miriam had forged. Why he wanted to cheat Gardner, I'll never know. I thought he would change if I gave him a chance. You see, I tried to burn the ledgers before my brother learned the truth. I never dreamed he would discover it in the ashes and blame Sundra!"

Instinct warned Gardner the situation was nearing a dangerous level even before Evans came scurrying back. The butler's message that Charles could not be found had quickly ignited speculations of alarm which sent the frightened women into hysterics.

"Silence!" Gardner demanded harshly, suddenly lowering his voice as he took James aside. "Hewett is after Sundra . . . I can feel it," he said, his body tense with flexed muscles. "By God, James, I've got to find her before anything happens to her, for reasons which you or Sir Edmund aren't likely to believe."

"Shall I ring the warning bell, Your Grace?" asked Evans, anxiously watching the duke and Sir James retrieving the pistols from the cabinet. He followed them into the foyer where canvas slickers were held ready by a footman.

"No . . ." came the response, cut short as Lieutenant Alexander and his two men were accompanying their screaming prisoner to the door.

"I wish I could be of help to you, Your Grace," said the lieutenant. "But I have a launch waiting to take us back to Amherstburg tonight. We must then set sail for England first thing in the morning."

"You've already been a great help to me, Alexander, and I thank you," replied Gardner, accompanying the men as far as the south gate.

Before Miriam was hauled into the boat, she trampled the ground, her black hair whipping in the wind as she fixed her hateful eyes on Gardner. "You'll pay for this," she hissed, wincing when the master-at-arms tugged at the irons securely locked around her wrists.

"When you reach Tyburn, m'lady, why not ask the devil if we haven't already paid dearly for our damnable actions," Gardner replied coldly, acutely aware of his own guilt. Never again would Sundra have to suffer because of his cursed pride and, if it wasn't too late to make amends, he'd gladly go alone to hell if given the chance to have his wife nestled safely by his side just one more time.

Fear constantly urging her onward, Sundra skirted the brittle scrub patches, too weary to notice if she had left a trail of footprints leading out of the hardwood forest. By now the rain was a steady downpour which shortened her field of vision. She more or less found the path leading to the east cranberry pond by sheer instinct.

Panting heavily, she managed to climb over a fallen tree and paused briefly to catch her breath. Her legs ached and the bottoms of her feet tingled from the chilled mud seeping into her frayed slippers. She might as well have worn nothing at all for what little protection her clothes provided her now.

Sundra forced herself to wade waist deep, crossing a stretch of marshland. She shivered more at the thought of stepping on unseen slimy creatures than she did for the bitter cold temperature of the murky water. "Dear Lord," she begged silently, "don't let anything grab hold of my legs, for they are too numb and I shall faint if I see something hanging onto me when I get out of this mess!"

Sundra reached higher ground and trudged southward, following the edge of the lake pond. It was when she tripped and fell close to a strand of pines that she decided she couldn't go on. As she crawled beneath a scented bough, her eyes filled with tears at the thought of being reduced to cowering like a frightened animal.

She huddled close to the only patch of dry ground the forest could offer. Her sense of hearing was the only tool of use to her during the dark and dreary night.

The rain tapered off to a light drizzle. Eventually, the moisture accumulated on the myriads of branches; dripping rivulets which made a plunk-and-thud sound as they fell to the pine-needled floor.

Sundra must have dozed off a dozen times against her will, only to be startledly awakened each time by a noise which ceased to exist once she became aware of it. Quietly she rolled away from her hiding place, shocked and alarmed to see a gray dawn breaking. Cautiously, she scanned between the evergreens and made a mental note to avoid the clearing beyond. "How could I have slept at a time like this!" she chided herself.

Keeping close to the black willows for cover, Sundra found her progress tediously slow, her legs straining to uphold her balance with each step she took in the ankle-deep muck. She had to repeatedly tug her skirt free from the drooping raspberry briers obstructing her path.

Just when Sundra thought she had penetrated deep into the wildwoods, miles of shoreline to her right and a barren strip of beach loomed unexpectedly into sight before her. She had unwittingly reached the southernmost tip of Point Pelee!

Backtracking was out of the question, she thought. Dare she linger out in the open, mindful of her dangerous stance as the waves kept crashing violently to shore?

Sundra's knees buckled and she sank dejectedly on a mound of sand. Slowly, as her eyes searched for a worthy hiding place, she became aware of wispy movements among the tree limbs covered with lianas of wild grapes and virginia creeper. She saw birds! A migration of delicate wings, too tired from migrating to preen their ruffled feathers.

The peaceful chirping was interrupted by the all too familiar shrieks of the whiskey-jays. Instinctively, Sundra scooted over to a clump of sawgrass too scanty of a cover for her to feel at ease. She waited, scarcely breathing, as she listened to something, or someone, trampling through the brush!

When she first heard the pathetic whine, her heart skipped a beat. Then, a couple of yelps led to a full outburst of eager barking. "Buster!" cried Sundra, scrambling to her feet. The dog's wagging tail gave her an exuberant welcome, but when she saw the leather strap tethered to a tree, restraining the terrier, she realized her mistake of throwing all caution to the wind.

It was time for Sundra to meet her fate; the world which had offered gaily-colored birds singing songs of hope had suddenly grown silent and forboding.

"Well played, Charles," she conceded grimly, painfully aware of his elongated shadow cast against the sand dune.

In answer, Charles merely snorted in disgust. "'Twas far from a game of wits, believe me," he scoffed arrogantly. "Had I known you'd be an easy catch, I would have blindfolded myself for the hell of it! Tell me, are you still happy to see that mongrel now that you've fallen for my trick? Oooh," he sighed regretfully, "I should have drowned the damned thing when I wanted to. Nothing would have given me greater pleasure than to have heard you shrieking your head off when you discovered him dead in your bed. At least Alice didn't disappoint me when she opened her soapbox. I've a passion for giving the oddest things, haven't I?" Charles smirked.

"I'm beginning to realize that nothing you do surprises me anymore," said Sundra flatly, "For once, I do hope Miriam turns greedy enough to cause your downfall."

Charles raised an eyebrow. "Dare you side with her after the way she's filched from you?"

Yes, thought Sundra, withholding her reply. At least Miriam is willing to spare Gardner's life! To comment now, she might force Charles's hand and jeopardize Gardner's future.

Buster was frantically pawing the ground, scattering dirt and leaves in his whiny struggle to break loose. His ear-piercing barks were carried away by the westerly gusts of wind.

"Oh, do be still," sputtered Charles, turning to give the dog a swift kick to the ribs.

Sundra saw her chance to escape and made a run for it, mindless that she was heading toward the barren tip that could offer her no form of protection. Her feet dug into the moist sand, and even before the twang of the vibrating bowstring could penetrate her thoughts, she knew it was too late! With a powerful jolt, the sharp-edged arrow swiftly pierced her back.

Sundra was too stunned to move or even feel the searing pain of a shattered shoulder blade. She dropped down on her knees, seeing and hearing nothing, her hands clenching fistfuls of pebbles in an effort to hold onto reality.

If this was the end, Gardner was all she wanted to think about. She knew he would eventually find her body and wondered if her diary would be enough to exonerate her from the wrongdoings he'd accused her of. It was a last wish of sorts that he should truly see her in a different light, far removed from the condemning shadow which had mistakenly been cast over her. Would it have mattered if she had confessed she loved him? Probably not, but now Sundra wished she had. "Oh, Gardner, I love you so," she whimpered softly.

"Oh, for heaven's sake, get up." Charles spoke impatiently. "See what you made me do? I missed a clean kill and it's all your fault!" Charles shook his finger in front of her nose, hauling her up by the arm. "Well, do be a good girl and stand still for me, would you? I wouldn't like to miss a second time."

"Why?" coughed Sundra, her right arm dangling useless by her side.

"Because I'd like to put an end to this silly game with a sure shot. Now, do you mind!"

"No, I mean, why do you want me dead?" Sundra had to know, regardless that Charles's patience was waning.

"Inheritance," he said simply. "First I took care of that brat Alice was carrying; 'tis only natural for you to go next. Gardner will soon follow you to your grave and then I can enjoy my estate with Alice . . . or perhaps Miriam," he pondered. "I haven't quite made up my mind which one I'll choose."

With courage Sundra never knew existed in her heart, she stood her ground and faced her executioner as he retrieved another arrow from the birch bark quiver. When Charles looked up, she saw the blood suddenly drain from his ruddy face.

"My God," he uttered in horror. "What is that thing!"

Bewildered, Sundra managed to look over her shoulder to see what had startled him. Nothing but sand was there, dashing her last hope of Gardner coming to her rescue.

Charles began walking backward, edging closer to the tip where dangerous undercurrents churned the surface of the water into frothy waves.

"Get back," he warned nervously. "Stay away from me, I tell you!"

He's gone mad, thought Sundra, quickly dropping to the ground when he let loose an arrow aimed at the unknown target behind her back. Within seconds he had expended all of the arrows on the empty beach.

Charles screamed in terror, flinging his bow to ward off an attacker whom only he himself could see. His hands clutched at his throat, his body struggling to keep from being dragged into the lake.

Sundra couldn't believe her eyes. Either Charles's capabilities for acting followed him into madness, or he was literally being lifted off his feet for a brief second by an invisible force. Frightened, she compassionately cried out for him to stop and come ashore.

"Help me," Charles sobbingly begged her.

No matter what Charles had tried to do, it wasn't in Sundra's nature to allow a helpless person's pleas go unheeded. Somewhere in the distance Sundra could hear her name being called to come away. Still, she persisted in trying to reach Charles and slumped forward, the arrow jutting out of her back causing excruciating pain to her body each time she clawed the beach to inch forward.

A mighty clap of thunder shook the land and then—all grew silent. Lake Erie had claimed Charles's life.

Sundra wept bitterly where she lay, darkness threatening to cover her mind as it had her eyes. She was in a deaf-mute state and felt herself being lifted up into warm, strong arms that held her securely. Lips too loving and gentle to be real caressed her cheek for an instant before she fainted.

The expression on Gardner's face was all James needed to swing into action, whipping his horse along the perilous trail to Tamarack to fetch Dr. Todd. He knew they would have to return in the supply boat not only because it was quicker but because Sundra would fare better in the transport.

Gently, Gardner laid Sundra on her left side and quickly built a bonfire on the beach to keep her warm and from lapsing into deep shock. He carefully dislodged the arrowhead, stanching the flow of blood with the only piece of clean material available—his silk shirt. With every anxious moment that passed he prayed for her, painfully aware Sundra might never know his true feelings for her. Gratefully, Gardner glanced at the feisty terrier lying next to Sundra. If it hadn't been for Buster's boisterous yapping, he and James would never have ventured to search this far down the Point.

It was a terrifying experience for Sundra to regain consciousness imprisoned in the arms of a man she couldn't see. She blinked in rapid succession to erase the haziness from her eyes, feeling a masculine hand pressing an easygoing restraint on her chest when she tried to sit.

"Charles, no!" she gasped in confusion. As she struggled to get up, the searing pain in her back crippled her movements. Her chin was uplifted against her will and, as her vision cleared, Gardner's face loomed welcomingly into sight.

"Be still," cautioned Gardner, his tone soft and comforting. "You're safe now, my love. Hewett will never hurt you or anyone else again."

Is this a dream, wondered Sundra, unable to believe that Gardner had come after her. Her lips moved, but she couldn't speak. All she felt was pain and a strange warmth from the giant flames leaping high into the somber sky—flames reminiscent of a funeral pyre which made her body suddenly shudder at the thought. An ebony veil darkened the sky, then slowly her eyes, and her mind drifted off again in unconsciousness.

Sundra's body and soul-searching thoughts were afloat in her dreamlike state, and she crossed the choppy waters of Lake Erie unaware, while Dr. Todd and Gardner kept a close watch over her.

They hardly more than touched shore when Evans, accompanied by a pack of able-bodied footmen, rushed up to the boat in their eagerness to lend a careful hand taking their mistress back to Tamarack. It was amazing how swiftly the truth had spread along the servant's grapevine. There wasn't a man among them who didn't feel shamefaced or guilty for having condemned his mistress' behavior of late. None the less, their mistake served as a valuable lesson, and they vowed forever to remain loyal to the duke and his innocent duchess.

Dr. Todd cleansed and stitched Sundra's wound and administered a strong dose of laudanum to induce a deep slumber for his restless patient. Squabbles forgotten, Mrs. McDewey and Addie pulled together their resources and fussed over Sundra during the next two days, nearly smothering her with attention in their attempt to get her back on the road to recovery.

The long hours spent confined to bed were not pleasant ones for Sundra. Charles's death was ever present in her mind during the day, nor, when the lengthening shadows covered the walls of her bedchamber, could she rest easy in the twilight, thinking about Miriam's tragic fate.

"A wave the size o' a tree swept her overboard," Addie had told her, repeating the story Lieutenant Alexander had given to the duke. "'Twas the strangest sight he e'er saw. Why, the waters of Erie was aboilin' and churning all around her, yet he says there wasn't a stormy wind ablowin' in the rain. The lake jest swallowed her up before the officer could jump in to unchain her wrists to rescue her. Miriam drowned like a rat, she did," said Addie, wide eyed and feeling gooseflesh prickling her chubby arms.

Mrs. McDewey and Addie quickly took advantage of the lifted restrictions and used the time ordinarily reserved for nursing to sit and chat with Sundra.

"Everyone wishes you well," they would chortle in unison. They dressed Sundra in lace bed jackets and brushed her hair, performing all the normal duties as beforehand with the exception of one important factor: they were acting out of character. Neither spoke her mind about the evil doings of Miriam and Charles, or the events which had brought Addie and Sir Edmund to Canada.

Sundra objected to being mollycoddled by the tight-lipped nannies. She had to know what had become of Alice and Gardner, especially Gardner, she thought, nervously winding a satin ribbon around her finger. What was he thinking about now that he'd rescued a wife who had flown from him? By all means he should be fit to be tied. Sundra had to admit, however, his feelings for her on the beach were far from being temperamental.

Gardner was gentle and protective. Since she hadn't seen him since the tragedy, she could only wonder where their love-hate relationship was leading them.

"Ouch," cried Sundra, raising her hand to rub her cheek which Mrs. McDewey felt the need to pinch.

"Now doon't ye look at me like that," scolded Mrs. Mc-Dewey. "I've got to put the color back in yer face somehow!"

"McDewey's right, child," added Addie. "How'll it look if ye still be as pale as a sheet after we've taken care of ye? And with visitors comin' to gawk at our pretty patient!"

Sundra sat at attention. Could this be the moment she'd been hoping for? Oh, Gardner, her heart called out to him. She blushed when she realized the two elderly women were staring at her.

"By all means, curl my hair, splash scented water on my wrists, and do whatever your little hearts desire," she laughed, lightly teasing them, "I'm feeling up to having a visitor!"

Finally, when there came a knocking at her door, Sundra was prepared. There was a certain excitement in the air and she felt enveloped by it as she eagerly said: "Come in!"

'Tis strange, thought Dr. Todd. The girl had been most anxious for callers, but now that he, James, and Sir Edmund were here, her lovely smile had suddenly vanished into thin air.

"Good afternoon, Sundra. You're looking very beautiful today," said James, noting Sundra's lips were slightly taut. "Obviously your eyes have much improved, for you to frown upon our beggarly faces," he chuckled.

"Aha!" remarked Dr. Todd, quickly cutting into the conversation. "You know Her Grace has had serious eye problems?"

"She met with an accident and was temporarily blinded," replied James matter-of-factly.

"Is that so?" gasped Sir Edmund. "Oh dear," he coughed. "For some reason or other, I'd thought she was suffering from some fatal malady back in England!"

"Indeed!" muttered Dr. Todd. "As a physician, the trouble marring Her Grace's eyes was the first thing I'd noticed when we first met. Been wanting to examine them ever since the duke and I concurred as to the nature of her problem."

Sundra flounced in bed, slamming her tiny fist against the satin coverlet. "Dr. Todd," she said shortly, thankful to be getting a word in edgewise. "Are you saying my husband told you that I was once blind?"

"But of course, m'lady," he replied. "Now, if you'll excuse me, I merely stopped by to give my regards before I take Sir Edmund on the grand tour of the infirmary. Are you ready, Dillingham?"

"Good day, your ladyship," they said, leaving Sundra to glower at James.

"Did you hear that!" she pouted. "All this time Gardner knew I was blind when I married him and yet, he never once told me that he knew. Oh, how arrogant of him! You can't imagine how miserable I've felt to think he never believed a word I said!"

"I can't blame you for being upset."

"Upset? Dear Lord, James!" replied Sundra, her eyes wide and sparkling with fire. "Have I been playing tug of war with my heart for nothing?" she cried. "I can't predict Gardner's change in moods from one minute to the next. Why, that man is impossible to live with!"

With his hand, James adeptly hid the smile playing on his lips before seriously replying: "If it's any consolation to you, Sundra, Gardner knew you were telling the truth from the very beginning, but, as you well know, he has a stubborn passion for not admitting his true feelings. Mind you, now, this doesn't mean I am condoning his behavior, or that I'm offering you an apology on his behalf."

"And I daresay I'll not hold my breath waiting for one to come from him," replied Sundra, pangs of sorrow tearing the inside of her heart. What must Gardner think of her after she told him those vicious lies in order to set him free and save his life? She would have been honored to abide by her husband's guidance, and to have his children—if only he'd love her.

"Well, I'm sorry to say that too many people have already muddled your life. You deserve better," said James, pulling out a long white envelope from his coat pocket. Tapping the edge against his palm, he eyed her seriously. "During my investigation in England, I discovered that all of Gardner's financial problems stemmed first from Charles, then from Miriam. Of course, I needed proof and Sir Edmund and Addie were only too happy to oblige me in the search, if it meant coming to Canada to see you again. Somewhere along the line Dilly got wind of your predicament and vowed to make it his business to correct at least his share of bumblings. This," he said, giving her the envelope, "is the result of a serious discussion Dilly had with Gardner. You are finally on your own to make what you will of it."

Quickly Sundra broke the seal, her hands trembling as she scanned the piece of parchment. "I don't understand," she said shakily, looking woefully up at James. "Gardner's given me an uncontested annulment document." Brushing a tear from her cheek, she took a deep breath, her heart pounding rebelliously against her thoughts of accepting the annulment. "Do you suppose you can manage to ask Gardner to come and see me? I don't think I'm asking too much now, do you?" she asked, a hint of sarcasm in her voice. If Gardner wanted to be rid of her, she wanted to hear it from his own lips!

"I'll try, although I can't promise when he'll be coming back to Tamarack."

"You mean he's . . . left home?" Sundra hurriedly asked in surprise.

"Didn't anyone tell you that Gardner was summoned to Fort Amherstburg early this morning?" asked James, yanking on his bothersome neckstock. "Lud!" he exclaimed loudly, breathing a deep sigh of relief. "No wonder you turned pale after I handed you those papers! You thought Gardner was making me do his dirty work for him, didn't you!" He smirked.

"You think this is amusing? Honestly, James, why do I always have to be the last to know what's going on around here? But tell me," she proceeded quickly, "why did he have to leave so suddenly?"

"There has been a murder allegation brought against him, and for once in his life, he's going to have to mind his manners in a court of law. 'Course, this doesn't mean it will stop Gardner from clashing with the governor in private."

"This is too serious to be a laughing matter," scolded Sundra, furiously twisting the covers. "Gardner could be sent to the gallows for all we know!"

"Hardly! I'm a witness to his innocence," James assured her, amazed at the intricate workings of a woman's mind. One minute Sundra was ready to let heads roll and the next, prepared to take up her husband's side during battle. "Women!" James retorted as though he objected to the word.

"And ye bawlin' men couldna live withoot us, to be sure," interrupted Mrs. McDewey, pushing her nose past the doorway. "Now if ye doon't mind, Jamie Moore, my Lady Alice has been pullin' oot her hair for a chance to visit with Her Grace."

Slowly Alice walked over to the mullion and turned to face Sundra, who had every reason in the world to hate her. She was contemplating making a run for the hallway, turning cowardly at the last minute, when Sundra's smile stopped her in her tracks.

"Come away from the window, Alice," Sundra beckoned softly. "I think it's time that we truly got to know each other, don't you?"

A second chance? Yes! Like a flood bursting forth, Alice suddenly let go of her strained emotions and wept openly as she ran eagerly to Sundra's bedside.

It was unfortunate for Gardner not to have made his position quite clear during the first day of discussion with the governor. Three drawn-out days later, he was still trying to take his leave, but Dorchester would not hear of it.

"Foxworthy, you've the devil chasing after you!" jested the governor. "How often do we get the chance to exchange words, especially since there's good cause for celebrating? Not only have you been cleared of murdering Adrian Shaw, you have proved your loyalty to your country beyond a shadow of a doubt by bringing the man responsible to justice."

"A mere stroke of luck, I assure you," answered Gardner shortly, taking his mind off Sundra long enough to contemplate the day's actions. It was by chance he and Fishbait Gilly had run into Deacon at the local tavern. Before long, Gilly had goaded an intoxicated Deacon into admitting that he was guilty of killing Shaw. Little did Gardner know that Gilly had been suspicious of Deacon, who was also wanted for instigating tension between the settlers and Indians. The governor swiftly dealt with Deacon and locked him up in the guardhouse after receiving a signed confession.

"Damn me, Gardner, I'd make light of your escapade of smuggling those retainers from Tyburn, if I knew you wouldn't unsheath your saber in a fit of quick temper," bantered Dorchester.

"All twelve men will make damned good Royal Canadian Volunteers," replied Gardner. "I had no idea they would turn themselves in for my sake."

"To be sure! They not only pledged their allegiance to serve this land, but saved your hide in the process."

"Then I shall take my leave, Dorchester," stated Gardner, "before you change your mind and prosecute me to the fullest."

During dinner at General Engmann's manor, Gardner's eyes narrowed in speculation. No doubt by now Sundra was up and walking the halls at Tamarack. It bothered him to no end that Sir Edmund and the cosseting maid's presence would be enough to influence Sundra's decision. They represented all that he had denied her: love and understanding. Now that he was committed here, he cursed himself for ever leaving without telling her how he truly felt. But surely it was too late for sentiments.

"What say you, Foxworthy? Can we make use of the *Windancer* tomorrow?" asked George, sloughing off Lucinda's reproachful stare. "Simcoe will be damned pleased to see us and, I might add, fortunate for us to inspect the road he's providing for our community with our financial supplements."

"By all means, do," Gardner drawled casually. "But you will have to give my regards to the lieutenant-governor, since I've made other commitments in the morning to settle Hewett's estate. As much as I've enjoyed your hospitality, I really must be returning to Tamarack after you've made use of my ship."

"What! And leave me alone to explain your absence to Dorchester? No thank you, Foxworthy," George replied haughtily, holding up his hands indifferently.

"A pox take you, George," fumed Lucinda, throwing her napkin on the table. "Are you forgetting that Gardner is newly married? He's probably anxious to keep his wife warm at night."

"Really, Lucinda! How you embarrass me," rasped the general.

Gardner pushed away from the table and scowled, prepared to retire for the evening. "Let me assure you that my return will be anything but heartwarming, believe me!"

It made no difference how long he'd been absent, conceded Gardner, whether he return home tomorrow or a week from now; the inevitable was sure to happen. Was it selfish of him to think it better to find the manor empty, rather than return in time to watch Sundra walk out of his life?

As if Hewett's disorganized last will and testament was not enough to tax Gardner's patience, a westerly was whipping the rain into particles of ice, causing concern that the tobacco hothouses might falter and fail during an attack of inclement weather.

To Gardner's surprise, a carriage stopped in front of the legal building. Lucinda appeared at the window, holding tightly onto her cloak and bonnet as the wind pushed her inside the office.

"I had a 'ell of a time getting here," yelled Lucinda, stamping the mud off her dainty boots.

Gardner offered to take her wet wrap and seat her near the glowing hearth, but she politely, if not emphatically, refused him.

"I didn't come for a social visit," she said shortly, "although heaven knows I could certainly stand your company. This letter arrived for you and it looked too important to just let it sit around until you came back for luncheon."

"I hate to sound ungrateful, Lucie, but you've come at a most inconvenient time. I should consider it lucky if I resolve this wretched mess within twenty-four hours."

"Pah! What could be more important than receiving a missive from Tamarack?" she asked impatiently. When the duke hastily seized the letter from her hand, she smugly added: "I knew you'd be interested!"

A swift glance told Gardner the letter was penned in James's handwriting. Frowning, he stood by the hearth and propped his arm on the mantle, his pulse quickening with every word he read:

> Foxworthy,
> As much as I would like to have cleared the air and part from you on friendlier terms, I cannot delay the *Northwind* any longer by merely waiting for you to return.
> Rest assured that Dillingham and Addie will see that all goes well on the journey back to England, where my duties now lead me. I share a great fondness for the Lady who caused us considerable concern in the past, and I will do everything in my power to ease the pain of leaving the land she had once hoped would be her new home. I won't deny my heart is committed to her.
> I know you would want her to continue sharing your home, but alas, the memories of Charles's and Miriam's death is too much for her to bear. I agree. Tamarack need not serve as a constant reminder of her shattered life. Perhaps this separation will help us put our lives in order.
> Undoubtably, you will find her farewell letter waiting for you. Read it immediately, before you make any more rash decisions.
>
> With sincere regards,
> James Moore

Too stunned to make a move, Gardner was at the mercy of his nagging conscience. He'd thought he had pretty well adjusted to the fact of consenting to the annulment if Sundra so desired. Well, she did, and now he realized it wasn't what he wanted her to do at all! He loved her, needed her, and his friend, damn him, was only too willing to take up with the only woman who ever really mattered in his life. Fool! He'd be damned if he was going to let Sundra go without putting up a fight to win her back!

"If that bastard thinks he's going to take what is mine, I'm going to wring his bloody neck!" threatened Gardner ominously, causing Lucinda to blanch.

"Lud, Gardner," exclaimed Lucinda. "Just whom are you going to throttle, and why?"

"I don't have the time or the patience to explain, Lucie," he replied, taking her by the shoulders as he pulled her toward the door. "I need a fast horse and I can't waste my time looking for one. Can you help me?"

"But of course! Take my outrider's mount. 'Tis one of the finest runners in George's stable. Do be careful," she added, too late for Gardner to hear, because he was heading out of Amherstburg at full gallop.

When the road ended, Gardner slowed the horse to a walk and entered the miserly trail. Aspen and birch grew in the damnedest places, he thought, hampering his progress through the forest. The sleet did not come pelting down as before, but the icy remains served as a reminder to tread cautiously on nature's slick pathway.

Gardner could not judge the time of day because the sun was blocked from view by a flotation of dismal clouds. Under stress and strain, he decided to disregard the elements and spurred his horse, racing recklessly to the shoreline.

Another half hour of hard riding and Gardner would be within the boundary of his estate. "Lord, if I should lose Sundra now . . ." he bellowed angrily to the merciless wind.

Both horse and rider showed signs of exhaustion and sweat as they hurdled fallen limbs, heedlessly charging headlong down a ravine as though they were devils hellbent on terrorizing the countryside.

Upon reaching the crest, Gardner did not hesitate to give the horse its lead. They descended another slope, sliding haphazardly until, unexpectedly, the horse's foot plunged into a fox-hole. Gardner was thrown off and tumbled head over heels down the rest of the steep incline. Screaming from a broken leg, the horse slithered after the duke, thrashing yet unable to get up on its feet.

It took a minute for Gardner to come to his senses, slapping broken twigs and leaves off his torn coat. The horse was moaning in agony. With a heavy heart, Gardner had to dispatch the fine animal to end its misery. 'Twas a sad ending, he thought gravely, admiring the horse for its stamina and the performance it gave while under the pressure of his ruthless commands. He was going to send someone to take care of the remains, rather than let the wolves feast on such a noble steed.

Gardner persevered, running, climbing, and walking fast-paced with all his strength to cover the remaining distance before he reached the end of his endurance. Branches slapped his face and the lowly brambles reached out with barbed tentacles to trip his feet. Whiskey-jays pierced the air with frightened cries, announcing his intruding presence with every grueling step he took.

The turbulent sound of water agitating the pebbled shore was music to his ears. Gardner was tense with excitement as he stumbled forward into the clearing, but his enthusiasm was cut short when he saw what Lake Erie had in store for him.

Three masts rigged with full sail bobbed five hundred feet away. Enraged, Gardner yelled at the top of his lungs. Suddenly four people ran to the ship's railing and waved to him. Gardner immediately recognized Sir Edmund and the portly Addie Quiggs. Alongside stood James and huddled in their midst was the young woman Gardner had come after! Never before had he felt so utterly helpless, watching in agony the ship slipping further away from shore.

Only after the ship was a mere speck on the horizon did Gardner budge from the beach, trudging dejectedly back to the manor. If only he could have had one last glimpse of Sundra's innocent face.

If Gardner expected the halls to be deserted, he was sadly

mistaken. As he entered the foyer most of the staff were clustered in groups, laughing and crying at the same time.

"Your Grace," announced Evans, dispersing the servants with deft movements of his gray eyes.

Mrs. McDewey came hobbling down the corridor and skidded to a halt. "Me goodness! Wot ye look at yerself," she scolded, "and forty minutes too late to say fare thee well to yer nice hooseguests!"

"I'm in no mood to tolerate the lash of your tongue, McDewey," growled Gardner, stomping off toward the study, only to find she had followed close behind.

"I doon't know wot's to become of yer temper," she remarked, shaking her head. "Here now, I think ye best read this."

Mrs. McDewey held out the scented letter for him to take. Without warning, Gardner slapped it out of her hand and walked away from where it lay on the floor.

Unaware of the duke's return, Coralee had seen Mrs. McDewey go into the study and skipped after her, tripping on the door jam and sprawling on the floor in a most unladylike position. Fluffing her petticoat, she looked up to find a pair of cold blue eyes reproaching her behavior.

"What the hell is she still doing here?" demanded Gardner.

"Who me?" squeaked Coralee. "Ribbons, Your Grace. I'm to fetch blue ribbons or none at all."

"Look in my sewing basket, child," whispered Mrs. McDewey, motioning for her to retreat quickly.

No doubt Alice had asked the girl to stay on, surmised Gardner, pouring a liberal portion of brandy into his glass. "McDewey!" he called. "Before you leave me in peace, see that Evans prepares a hot bath for me," he commanded, slipping off his boots.

"Well ye'll joost have to wait! M'lady is still soaking in it," she replied haughtily, slamming the door behind her.

"Damn it!" scoffed Gardner. Was he not lord and master of his own home? 'Twas bad enough the servants seemed hellbent on revenge for the way he had treated Sundra, without his sister trying to domineer his life too! Tomorrow he'd straighten things out in a hurry!

Gardner stared into the roaring fire, aware the house was deathly quiet now that the servants had retired for the night. It was ironic he should feel the need for a comforting shoulder now that he was left alone with his thoughts. The four walls seemed to be closing in on him. Without Sundra, Tamarack had lost its glitter. The place was nothing but a mere shell, like his heart, and he had only himself to blame for causing his great sorrow.

Plagued with a splitting headache, Gardner leaned back on the cushion, allowing his arms to dangle wearily over the sides of the armrests. A cold, wet nose suddenly pushed against the palm of his hand. With a muffled snort, Buster pranced on the floor when his master rewarded him with a pat on the head. "You miss her too, eh?" he asked.

Gardner wondered if he'd be satisfied to live with mere memories. Or should he sail to England and persuade her to come back? Perhaps he'd know where he stood once he got up enough nerve to read her letter. Knowing Sundra, the words would probably be as kind and gentle as the lady who wrote them.

Gardner knew something was wrong the minute he retrieved the letter, but couldn't imagine what it was until the scent drifted up toward his nostrils. Roses! Only Alice wore that scent! Why would Sundra not use her own haunting lily-of-the-valley perfume?

Buster persisted in tugging at Gardner's sleeve and he had to push the little dog off his lap before he could tear open the letter. Buster ferociously growled back at him.

"Who let you in here anyway?" asked Gardner, watching the dog prick up his ears.

"I did," replied a timorous voice.

Was he imagining he heard Sundra's voice? Without a second thought Gardner flew out of the chair and faced the doorway. "My God," he said deeply, "but I saw you . . . leave . . . how ᵈⁱᵈ " stammered the duke.

Sundra lovingly shook her head and smiled, tears flowing down her cheeks as she rushed into his arms. She clung tightly to him and returned his rapturous kisses with an eager passion of her own.

Sundra felt crushed by Gardner's embrace, yet, she would not have their reunion any other way as long as she could revel at the tumultuous pressure of his heart beating closely to hers.

"I love you," he announced for all the world to hear, picking her up and twirling her around with his arms clasped tightly around her waist.

The glint in his eyes told Sundra he had indeed noticed the blue negligee that at one time he had offered his pair of matched bays to see her wear.

"I should have known you'd never leave me, but I was too afraid to even hope such a thing when I noticed the perfume on the letter was not yours," said Gardner.

"Mrs. McDewey told me you'd be too angry to read Alice's letter. I tried to come to you as quickly as I could," she said, finding her way back into his loving arms. "James was quite smitten with your sister, but I don't suppose you ever took the time to notice."

"One fault of many, I assure you, and tomorrow you may correct me on every count," he teased, feeling her gentle hands caressing the back of his neck. "You've played a dangerous game by hiding upstairs while you must have known I was suffering down here in hell."

"Let me remind you, sir, that I came to repay my debts to you as fast as I could. You rescued me a second time from Point Pelee, for which you demanded a kiss in return for your courageous services. Now I ask you," she murmured coyly, snuggling contentedly closer against his chest, "wasn't it worth the wait?" Before Gardner could answer, Sundra's lips offered its sweetness to his demands.

"Ah yes, m'lady," he whispered huskily in her ear, placing an intimate kiss on the gentle swell of her breast as he swooped her up into his arms to hold her possessively close. "Just to feel you in my arms again was worth the anticipation."

Gardner gave her a desirous grin and ardently carried Sundra to the winding staircase.

"And now, my love, I will show you there is yet another pleasure well worth waiting for."

Berencsi
Wildwoods and wishes

FL 97041

E

		DATE DUE		